Tony Peake was born in South Africa. He now lives in London, where he works as a literary agent. His first novel, *A Summer Tide*, was published last year.

Seduction

A book of stories

Edited by
TONY PEAKE

Library of Congress Catalog Card Number: 93-86624

A catalogue record for this book is available
from the British Library on request

First published 1994 by
Serpent's Tail, 4 Blackstock Mews, London N4
and 401 West Broadway #1, New York, NY 10012

Typeset in 10½/13pt Palatino by Servis Filmsetting Ltd.
Printed in Great Britain by Cox & Wyman Ltd.,
of Reading, Berkshire

Contents

Introduction

The archetypal seduction story – certainly the most potent and evocative – has to be that of Ulysses and the siren. It contains all the basic ingredients: the awful power one person can exert over another, how that power can trick you off course, and how willingly – unless there's an accomplice on hand to lash one to the mast – a person will abandon everything to follow the lure of the siren.

In my travels round the Mediterranean, I have had more than one rock pointed out as the site of the legend, and in Italy, on the Amalfi coast, I was told with great authority that the siren's song was nothing more than the call with which the local shepherds rounded up their goats. From the sea, my informant explained, this shepherd's song sounds positively ethereal.

The truth, of course – as the stories in this collection so vividly demonstrate – is that the rock is anywhere and everywhere, the song not necessarily melodious, the siren as various as her prey. All that is required is a listening ear.

Tony Peake

Soft Sell – a Fantasy

A . L . B A R K E R

After the publication of her definitive history of seduction, detailing sexual practices from Cro-Magnon to Common Market man – the habits and compulsions of lower animals, courtship displays, arousal emissions and the adhesive methods of molluscs, right down to basics such as the stimulation of gonads – Atlanta rated a comprehensive entry in a directory of exceptional women. She was ill-advised to permit the inclusion of her private address. A direct result was an increase in unsolicited mail, but she had always been a hard touch and continued to drop everything straight into the pedal bin.

There was of course no discrimination in the offers and incitements which came through her letterbox. As the author of a work of scholarship on a vital theme she resented being classed in the same catchment area as women who fretted about getting their carpets cleaned and converting their kitchens to stripped pine. She took even greater exception to the tone of some of the charitable appeals. Tiresome and sometimes sickening details were accompanied by a row of boxes stipulating the amount to be donated, from £5 to £10,000 ('other' in small print was plainly intended to be shaming) by standing order, or deed of covenant.

Atlanta's flush of youth had faded long since. She forbore to tint her hair and did nothing about her face which was jowly and rather Tudor; she sometimes caught Henry Five looking at her out of the mirror. She dressed sensibly and warmly because eccentric or flamboyant clothes did not become her and because she felt the cold.

She was not cold by nature. It went without saying, she had been known to say, that heart as well as intellect was essential to the understanding of her subject. Seduction, however engineered, cannot succeed without a nucleus of love. Lecturing on the art of the embrace, she maintained that the seducer must be a teeny-tiny bit at the mercy of the seduced, and here her confederate twinkle always sent a ripple through the audience.

She could still enjoy a conquest, though it was a long time since she had made one. Putting herself out to the necessary extent had become more of a chore than a challenge. It was nothing to do with age, except for that pearl of wisdom about custom staleing infinite variety which was, after all, simply the price of experience.

She was not without inclinations; it would have been worrying if she were. There was a personable young creature working on a block of flats being built opposite her own. The weather being warm, he stripped to the waist. She watched through opera glasses the synchronizing of his back muscles as he went up and down ladders carrying a hod, and fantasized about the motion of his skin under her fingers. But her pleasure was largely academic; she realized that close acquaintance would disappoint, she observed that he indulged in horseplay and had a vulgar laugh.

A more promising proposition was a man who hosted one of the literary chat shows on TV. He was older, urbane, trendily but tastefully dressed, had silver sideburns and a heart-stopping mouth. Atlanta hoped to meet him. It was surely unnecessary to point out to the programme makers what a draw she would be, how her

specialized knowledge would capture every class of audience; serious, salacious and incurious. She waited in the
confident expectation of being invited to take part in the
chat. Meantime, the host was her weekly date with the
box, she missed nothing of him: the shine on his lips, the
plumpness of his ear-lobes, the mount of Venus at the base
of his thumb. Such particulars fuelled the thoughts which
she took into her bed. And her dreams. But it should not
be supposed that she was lovesick; advancing years
merely added spice to the challenge.

The Catalogue arrived one day while she was out. She
found it propped against her street door. It measured a
foot square, half an inch thick and weighed one and three-
quarter pounds. Incredulous, she weighed it. The accom-
panying letter described it as the 'curriculum vitae of a
superior lifestyle, featuring fabulous creations of talented
craftsmen, gifts for the discriminating, rare antiques,
flawless jewels, vintage wines, Florentine leather goods,
incunabula, and curiosa'. The letter went on to say that in
addition to high-altitude merchandise this House offered
a unique range of services destined for 'the lotos-eater
and the motivated alike', and could assist in 'procuring' –
here Atlanta's eyebrows rose – the object of any desire
'however unusual'. There followed a guarantee of
absolute discretion and an assurance that at no time
would any detail of a customer's order be made public.

'Well, what do you know?' Atlanta asked herself. Like
many people living alone she occasionally gave voice to
her extremes of feeling. On this occasion she supplied a
Rabelaisian reply. Then she began to leaf through the
Catalogue.

It was far from being the usual mail-order format.
Bound in white board with Gothicized lettering embossed
in gold, the pages on quality gloss, impeccably printed,
richly coloured or, where more appropriate, in dignified

monochrome, it was a presentation such as Atlanta would have welcomed for her own work.

The articles and services on offer were so extraordinary as to cause her to blink. Not only were they artfully displayed, but each was described in offbeat poetic prose with sufficient technical data to intimidate the lay person. The whole thing was done with pizzazz and an effrontery which first impressed Atlanta, then put her back up. The postmark was Oxford, well-heeled city with sub-cultures quite capable of launching this self-styled 'life-enhancing document'.

Familiar though Atlanta was with the fatuities of *homo sapiens*, the Catalogue diverted her. It diverted her from the draft of her new book, provisionally titled 'An Investigative Account of the Awful Revelations of Maria Monk – sexology in medieval monastic houses'. She found herself speculating on the genuineness of the offers. How would it be if she applied to join the session on the acquisition of self-knowledge, 'conducted in the intimate ambience of a moated grange'? Or sent for the 'fully authenticated electroplate reproduction of the Cellini Salt Cellar' – on approval or return? In a spirit of empiricism she wrote for details of the hang-gliding course.

A few days later she was taking a nap when the bell rang. She ignored it. Someone put a finger on the bell-push and leaned on it. She rose up in a rage, went to the door with hair mussed, a superannuated wrap over her shoulders, wearing the horn-rims with which she replaced her contact lenses when she was alone.

She was to regret it. That first impression, she came to believe, sealed her fate.

'Good afternoon.' He made a charmingly ineffectual gesture as if to remove his hat which he was not wearing. 'May I speak with your daughter, Madame?'

'I have no daughter.' Atlanta's tone was frosty though her feelings were calorific.

'Your niece?'

'I have no niece.'

'Then I have come to the wrong address. I search a Miss Atlanta' – there followed an anxious patting of his pockets, accompanied by a translucent smile, rueful and sweet. 'Pardon, Madame, I have forgotten – '

'I am she.' Atlanta was dissolving into something rich and far from strange. It was the same old magic changing her flesh from a solid buttress to a pillar of fire. It was Inclination in the positive and delicious sense.

This young man was most certainly delectable, and he was on her doorstep. She said, 'What can I do for you?' resisting an urge to rephrase the question.

'Is it you, Madame, who asks particulars of our hang-gliding course?'

He sounded incredulous, as well he might. He also sounded foreign, French or German. His were the blond curls and scissor legs of a young gauleiter.

'Yes, it was me.'

'I have not understood. Your pardon, Madame, I must not presume –'

'No, you mustn't.' She had a wild wish that he would, then and there, on the doorstep.

He looked anxious. 'I am sent by my Company to inquire into your desires' – at that Atlanta gave him one of her baroque glances – 'in the matter of hang-gliding,' he said, round-eyed.

'You'd better come in.'

It took a high hand and sorcery to carry off the next ten minutes. She offered him tea, which he refused: whisky he also refused. He sat on the edge of a chair, his lap full of literature – Atlanta glimpsed a photograph of someone in a harness attached to a huge kite.

He began his recital: 'This most delightful sport you have chosen combines adventure with the serenity and beauty of a bird's flight, prospects of countrysides as seen from a bird's eye, it is a deeply satisfying and sustaining exercise, greatly favoured by executives wishing to escape the pressure of business.'

'I'm not escaping from anything, but if I am to fly like a bird and see like a bird I'll surely end up with a brain like a bird's.'

A lovely little tuck appeared between his eyebrows. He had heavenly eyebrows, wide-swept like – yes, the wings of a bird, a seagull. Or a condor, she thought madly.

He said, 'Have you read our testimonial?'

'I've glanced.'

'It will repay more than a glance. We can supply exquis-ite objects, fabulous creations of the world's craftsmen, gifts for the discriminating, antiques, Florentine leather, exotic perfumes, rare wines – '

'Life-enhancing stuff.'

'The vee on rose,' he said quaintly, 'is for those who appreciate it.'

Atlanta thought he's not foreign, it's all put on. She said, 'Why me?'

'You were selected from our Prestige Customer file.'

'I get loads of junk mail, it goes straight into the bin.'

'Is our merchandise junk?'

His dander was up. Atlanta had never been clear what a dander was, but the word suited his display of pique. When his eyes flashed and his lips pouted, she felt quite dizzy.

'I didn't say that. I'm talking about canvassing by dou-ble-glazing firms, and carpet shampooers. And demands for funds to support addicts and recidivists and victims of man's inhumanity to pussies, donkeys and pre-packed parakeets.'

'These too are junk?'

'My heart bleeds, but there's a limit to the heart's blood. I need to conserve mine, I work hard.'

'You should take a holiday. Sun and sea: Baku in the spring – see the Shah's palace and the Virgin's Tower and the oil-wells. Or ride on a dromedary across the Sahara to the Tibesti Mountains. We can offer a Roman villa on a Mediterranean island complete with sudatorium – a room where you go to sweat.'

'I do know,' Atlanta said sharply, 'but I don't like holidays.'

He stood up. 'Madame, I am wasting your time.'

'For heaven's sake stop calling me Madame! You know my name, I don't know yours.'

He bowed. 'Rudolf.'

'I can't call you that. There's a ridiculous rhyme about a reindeer.'

His smile sent frissons along her spine. 'Call me Freddy.'

'I'd like to see your jewellery. You may bring a selection for me to look at tomorrow. At three o'clock. I have a penchant for diamonds.'

She had her hair washed and set bouffant style which, though largely superseded, had suited her in the past. It gave her something of a bubble look but she concluded that was due to the floaty feeling she had. She managed to get into a crimson moiré dress, last worn in the seventies. The colour was right, but the neckline prudish, so she slit it: ripeness being all, she had no worries about her cleavage.

He came. He had everything going for him, youth, looks – and chastity. He appeared on her doorstep, as fresh as a daisy. Not for the first time, though she had known him rather less than half an hour, she longed to take him in her arms. It would have been an aborted move, he was holding to his chest a slender case in crocodile maroon.

'Do sit down.' When he went to a chair she cried, 'Not there, let's sit together on the settee. Then you can show me what you've brought.'

Beside him, their shoulders touching, was the moment she had been waiting for.

'Diamonds are your preference you said, Madame.'

'I asked you not to call me that.'

'It is a condition of the Company – '

'You're not with the Company now, you're here with me. Alone.'

She wondered afterwards if the moment she had been waiting for was one he had been ready for because he moved out of contact, gently, as if from a forward child.

'Isn't there a saying that diamonds are forever?'

Atlanta was annoyed but knew better than to show it. She said, 'What's in the case?'

He opened it with a reverence which was doubtless also a condition of the Company. Inside, each in its own velvet-lined compartment, was a dazzling array of jewellery. Atlanta was dazzled despite herself. She took the opportunity of closing the gap between them, it was reasonable to suppose that she wished to look closely at the merchandise.

He began: 'Platinum is used for many of our pieces, it is one of the rarest metals, and the purest for ornamental jewellery. Here is a gold-enamelled bracelet set with diamonds. The design is futuristic, the work of a leading craftsman in the field – '

'I hate spiders.'

'Spiders?'

'I certainly wouldn't wear them on my wrist.'

'The design is of spinning comets. But perhaps you prefer a slave bangle of platinum with a simple motif of black opals.'

'I have never been anyone's slave.'

'I believe your birthstone is the garnet?'

'How do you know?'

'Our Prestige Customer file carries such details as enable us to ensure the utmost satisfaction of our clientele.'

'Exploitation of my intimate personal details will not contribute to *my* satisfaction!'

'The month's all I know, not the year.' It was roughly spoken, in contrast to the routine he had learned by heart. He quickly recovered himself. 'What about this drop pendant – nine carat gold set with garnets and freshwater pearls? There's an eighteen inch chain' – he flashed a panicky glance at her cleavage – 'to go round your neck.'

'It's fogyish.'

'This beautiful Cleopatra necklet in gold? Or a lapel pin with a design of a pierced heart, a retainer is supplied without extra charge.'

'You must be thirsty trotting out all this expertise.' Ignoring his disclaimer, she fetched two large whiskies. She pushed one into his hand. 'Put down the case and relax.'

'You are not interested in these wonderful jewels?'

'Where are you from?'

'From?'

Bethnal Green I'd say, she thought, but something – that modicum of love perhaps – stopped her saying it. 'You're not French and you're not German. You're a clean-limbed English boy.'

She put her hand on his knee. He gulped the whisky with what might have been long practice, except that he immediately went into a paroxysm of gasping and coughing.

'I saw nothing in this to tempt me.' She removed the case from his lap, put an arm round his shoulders and massaged the small of his back. 'Take a deep breath, relax.'

He turned to her, tears stood on his cheeks, a ringlet clung damply to his brow. 'Where did I go wrong?'

'You drank too fast.'

'I have not tempted you!'

'Oh but you have. Not with the jewellery, though.' She let her hand travel to the nape of his neck.

'You do not wish to buy?'

She wound one of his curls round her finger – as she had been longing to. 'Interest me in something else.'

'I do not know your tastes.'

'Didn't your Prestige Customer file tell you I am a historian of evolution – from the first throbbing in the mud to our own full-blooded passions?'

They were knee to knee, thigh to thigh. He had begun to tremble, which was promising.

'We have a witness to the history of life, a primeval lizard executed in gold leaf on a blue velvet plaque. I recommend it,' he said quaintly.

'You mean I should hang it on the wall, like a moose head?'

'Furs, perhaps? We could show you dyed Canadian squirrel, blue with autumn highlights. Or musquashes of perfect quality, cut in the height of fashion.'

'Aside from humanitarian grounds I could not put them next my skin. They're rodents.'

'A set of treen tableware, authentic copies of the eating and drinking vessels used by medieval monasteries?'

'Ah.' Though momentarily arrested by this reminder of her current work, Atlanta was aware of a struggle going on between their nether regions. 'Horribly unhygienic,' she said sharply.

'You do not keep servants?'

'I gave them the afternoon off because I wished to be private.'

'Thus you would find a robot useful.'

'A what?'

'A mechanical servant to do for you in fullest confidence. He can be programmed in advance, the functions of head, arms, wrists and fingers remotely controlled. Our model embodies a cassette and can speak, a constant companion and willing slave. He will recall your appointments, wake you and serve your morning tea and take messages over the telephone.'

'I have an ansafone. The other things I prefer to do for myself.'

The disagreement between their pelvic girdles intensified, his trying to get away, hers to stay close. Convulsive movements had worked her skirt up to her knees, an elasticated knicker-leg was showing. She knew that she held a good hand, but it was possible to overplay it. She stood up, smoothing her skirt.

'I'm thinking of buying a car. My lecture tours take me all over the country. I need something dependable with limited stress factor.'

He retrieved his case and sat gripping it between his knees. For the first time he expressed reservation: 'I'm afraid our cars are designed for the enthusiast with a taste for speed and skilled in handling automotive power.'

'Road-hogs in other words. I too need speed, time is of the essence.' She was the career woman, lighting a cigarette. 'What do you suggest?'

A moment elapsed while his mind almost visibly turned to a new page of the Catalogue. 'Our series features 3.5 litre engines, a close-ratio gearbox, limited slip differential, asbestos-free brake pads with optimum retardation, 62 m.p.h. acceleration in seven seconds and a top speed of 140.' The recital was delivered in a monotone, he was sulking.

'What about comfort?'

'All the cars have air-conditioning, tinted windows with automatic winders, sapele wood instrument panels and electronically operated reclining seats in buffalo leather.'

'I'll take a test drive. Tomorrow.' Atlanta made a show of looking at her watch. 'Now I must ask you to leave, I have an engagement.'

He stood up. 'I will arrange for someone to come and demonstrate the car.'

'You must come yourself. I have no intention of changing my salesman at this stage.'

'It may not be possible for me – '

'You or no one.' She made an ushering gesture. 'I shall be waiting.'

It rained next day. At four o'clock exactly the car drew up, viper-green with chromium flashes shimmering under raindrops. It slid into the kerb, smooth as a monster surfacing from the deep. Atlanta, whose tastes inclined elsewhere, could appreciate the lust it aroused in men. Perhaps even in some women, she thought as she sank into the buffalo leather behind a dashboard studded with delicately quivering dials, an adjustable vanity mirror, and glove compartment bearing the word HERS in silver filigree.

Freddy had recovered his spirit. The car excited him. It caused her quite a pang to see how tenderly he took the wheel in his hands, stroked it round corners, holding and prizing it. They inched through the traffic to the river, crossed, and made better time on the Surrey side.

'Where are we going?'

'To the motorway so I can let her out.'

Atlanta had been hoping for a fine day to dally by a river or couch among the bluebells. The windscreen wipers fanning to and fro mesmerized her. She closed her eyes, opened them as the car suddenly surged forward. She was looking at a six-lane highway.

Freddy cried 'Now!' With the sound of a deep organ note the car leaped into the middle lane. Freddy's hands closed fiercely on the wheel. They shot round a container-lorry into the third lane. Freddy laughed with a boy's joy. 'Ninety!'

Exhilarated, Atlanta cried 'Faster!' A needle climbed steadily on the dash. Rain sheeted down the windscreen, the car's voice settled to the hum of a hive of bees. 'One hundred and twenty!' cried Freddy. 'How's that?'

'Faster! I'm not called Atlanta for nothing!'

His knuckles shone white on the wheel. 'We're over the limit, not of what this car can do, but of the margin of safety.'

Atlanta felt a sinking in the pit of her stomach as the car slowed, but she loved it when he was masterful and caring. They infiltrated the slow lane and took a left turn off the motorway. He pulled into a lay-by. 'Do you want to try her?'

'I'd like to try the reclining seats.' Atlanta had never owned a car and couldn't drive.

He leaned across, touched a lever on the dash and she was gently lowered, with a whiff of buffalo, to a relaxed position under his elbow. His face was close enough for her to see tomorrow's gold stubble peeping out of his pores. It made her feel quite weak, but not so weak that she couldn't reach up to draw his face down to hers.

As a caress it was a failure. Their noses collided: hers, being the bonier, came off best.

'Not here!' He picked her hand off the back of his neck. Next moment she and her seat were returned to the upright, the engine switched on and they moved away at speed.

'Where are we going?'

'Back.'

He was of course quite right. Anything achieved in a lay-

by off a busy road would be fragmentary at best. That he
was shy was part of his charm, that he was innocent was
the essence of it. Her privilege would be to enlighten him.

Driving past the Happy Eaters and baronial hyper-
markets of rural Surrey, she rehearsed the sequence of
events when they would have returned to the flat.

'What do you think?' he said.

'It will be heavenly.'

'Yes, it is a heavenly car.'

The rain was easing off by the time they got to West
One. He pulled into the kerb with a rich swish of tyres. 'I
am so happy you are pleased.'

She laid her hand on his. 'We must talk.'

He got out and came round to open the car door. 'Now
that you have decided to buy the car, the transaction will
be the responsibility of another department. A member of
our finance staff will call on you.'

'I have not yet decided.'

'In that case, Madame, I shall leave you to think about
it.' His tone was crisp, he slammed the car door, did a stiff
little bow from the waist. 'I must return to the garage.
Another client awaits.'

'May I remind you that *I* am your client and I have not
yet dispensed with your services.'

'I fear I can offer nothing more of interest to you.'

'You underestimate yourself, and me. Your Company
proposes a wide range of services and I intend to avail
myself of one of them.' He leaned against the car, looking crumpled. She said firmly, 'I wish to engage a
companion.'

'A companion?'

'Yourself, in fact.'

'Madame!'

'Don't call me that!'

'It is not possible what you ask!'

'Listen to me. Your Catalogue expressly states that customers' wishes will be met, however extraordinary they may be. I quote: "We will make possible for you anything which is possible at all".'

'But I cannot become your companion – I have my life – '

'I ask it for this evening only. I shall of course pay whatever fee is required.'

'But it is contrary to Company rules. Members of staff may only be employed by clients in an advisory capacity – '

'I haven't specified in which capacity I propose to employ you.' A glazed look came into his eyes. His jaw dropped and his mouth opened, he appeared quite stupid. Atlanta had no compunction in saying, 'You realize I could make things difficult for you? I need only mention your inconsiderate behaviour, cursory treatment, and hint at your unwelcome advances.'

'I would deny everything!'

'I rather fancy my reputation as a historian and my status as a Privileged Customer would invalidate your denials.'

'Why are you doing this?'

'Because you have not realized my wishes.'

The amber street lighting gave a general glow, rain fell in fiery particles, but he had no effulgence now, even his hair was damped down. 'I have done all that you asked.'

'I'm asking for the pleasure of your company this evening. Surely that is not an unreasonable request.'

'I have another engagement – '

Atlanta said, 'I shall be waiting for you.'

Dinner would have been an interruption, she decided against it, replenished the whisky decanter but did not put out nuts or crisps: the spirit would the sooner inspirit an empty stomach.

It was longer than she cared to remember since she had been in this happy situation of awaiting a lover. However, she remembered what was due to the occasion, bathed with a liberal addition of perfumed oil, loosed her hair and got into a peignoir.

She did her nails while she waited, they were still wet when the bell rang. He had come early. She went to the door waving her fingers to dry the varnish.

A giant of a man holding a wooden crate in his arms said, 'Miss Lanter?'

'I beg your pardon?'

'Merchandise as ordered.'

'I have not ordered any merchandise.'

'Special delivery to Miss Atta Lanter at this address.' He peered at her. 'You a white African?'

'Certainly not! My name is Atlanta – '

'That's what I said. Sign here. The invoice is inside the box.'

'But I haven't – '

'As a Privileged Customer you have the option of returning the goods within fourteen days if not fully satisfied. But the batteries must be intact.'

'Batteries?'

She was gazing at the box in his arms. Across the top were stencilled the words: 'Freddy, Your Faithful Robot'.

The Blue Woman

MARY FLANAGAN

Even when he was drunk, Malcolm's sense of direction was infallible. In fact drink seemed to enhance his gift for finding the right street in a sixteenth-century urban maze, the dirt track whose entrance lay shrouded in fog and brambles, the only tourist-free restaurant in the middle of July. Jane, who could not drive in London and frequently became disorientated in her own neighbourhood – never mind Xania – trusted absolutely in his instincts.

'I have no space perception,' she would sigh.

'But you have other strengths,' he'd console.

She did. Though Malcolm drove like a professional and excelled at water sports, his position on the magazine was less secure than Jane's who had been there four years and was in line for deputy editor. This state of affairs bred a resentment he worked hard to suppress but which surfaced occasionally when his competitive parts were pricked. Jane found these efforts admirable, endearing even.

They discussed professional matters over a dinner of fish soup with potatoes, onions and diverse marine life eaten at a table by the edge of the black satin sea. The restaurant was the last – and the best – on the port with its loops of lights strung along the curved Venetian harbour. Another of Malcolm's famous discoveries and the only place at which all the clientele were Greek.

She was reminding him that no one could afford to spend money on advertising now. Although readership was up, net income was down. It was the recession. If the magazine made cuts it wasn't personal.

'I don't think we should talk about work,' said Malcolm.

'Neither do I. Oh this is so delicious.' Jane ladled a second helping from the steaming soup pot. 'You too?'

'Yes please. Another bottle of retsina?'

'Definitely. But let's get the one with the cap not the cork. I'm learning to love the taste of turpentine.'

'You just like it rough,' he teased.

'Sometimes.' For a moment she relished an imaginary danger.

They smiled and held each other's gaze.

They enjoyed looking at each other. Why shouldn't they? At thirty they could easily pass for twenty-five. They swam and went to the gym. They ate sensibly but well and, though they worked hard, had time to enjoy themselves. Their salaries were about the same, Jane having a slight edge. (Mal attributed the discrepancy to a tacit antagonism between the editor, Justin, and himself.) Both assumed they were en route to successful media careers. Occasionally each suspected that they might be more intelligent than the other, but these thoughts were never expressed and the general impression was that theirs was an entirely equal partnership.

Their affair was approaching that apogee which occurs at six months and is sustained for perhaps another two or three before reaching the straight gate at which it either terminates or attains a higher, if less intense, emotional plateau. Malcolm and Jane did not think about this sad but inevitable transition. Why should they? They hadn't even begun to exhaust their supply of jokes and endearments. Hundreds of biographical anecdotes waited in their mutual wings. They were still a mystery to each other. Small wonder London-bred anxieties had made few raids on their exclusive holiday happiness.

When they had finished the soup they lingered a while, looking across the port to the causeway where pedestrians strolled. They fed the one-eyed cat, held hands across the table and took turns rubbing their toes against each other's ankles.

'You're so beautiful,' said Mal. 'You're all shining.'

When they rose to leave Jane extended her hand, palm up.

'Take me somewhere,' she said.

Inside the city, away from the water and the breeze, it was hot. Even at midnight the temperature hung in the high eighties.

The crowded arteries were busy and bright with the restaurants and shops where tourists idled. Human voices echoed off the cobblestones of narrow passageways. Music from several opposing bouzoukis collided overhead where bright stars were visible even through the competition of so much electricity. The smells of cooking, the laughter of children, the octopuses drying on the backs of chairs: stereotypical Greece at the height of stereotypical summer. But no less lovely for that, agreed Malcolm and Jane.

Simultaneously they stopped to admire a scarified pink and yellow wall that looked like an abstract painting.

'You give such wonderful hugs,' murmured Jane as they held each other.

'I love to hug you,' replied Mal gallantly.

'Why?' she laughed, but he was very serious.

'Because it makes me feel I really have you and that I can't lose you.'

'You can't lose me.' She liked that he was strong enough to admit his insecurities.

They edged gradually towards the darker fringes of the city.

'Look at him!' Jane pointed at a gigantic cockroach making its insolent way along the pavement.

'In Mexico they're even bigger,' Mal assured her.

As they spoke a lithe little cat sprang out of the night, snatched up the cockroach and trotted proudly off, the insect's feet waving between her jaws.

'Excellent,' said Malcolm.

'Absolutely,' said Jane. And for a while they discussed the agility and resourcefulness of cats. Both were confirmed ailurophiles. It was one of the many things they thought they had in common.

They walked on, hand in hand. They were in no particular hurry. Malcolm was taking them somewhere. Though he was not yet sure where that somewhere might be, he knew it was out there, waiting for him. He could smell it, and was following his brilliant nose.

'Mal's at his best when he's travelling,' Jane would tell her friends. 'Everything with Mal's a big adventure and he finds all the best places, secret places the tourists miss or are too lazy to look for. I suppose a lot of it is experience,' she'd amend. 'Mal's certainly been around.' She was proud of Malcolm.

They had come to a very old part of town. Cooking aromas no longer hid the underlying smell of decay that seeped from ancient foundations and from the rows of long tubular boathouses where the Venetians had once dry-docked their beautiful ships and which were now warehouses or watermelon depots or else stood empty. Street lamps and pedestrians became infrequent. Rubbish lay in heaps beside the houses.

'Oh goodie,' said Jane. 'We're lost.' And they stood for a moment relishing their directionlessness. Then from a distance came the sound of Cretan music – authentic

Cretan music, not the Westernized sort that was pumped from loudspeakers at Zorba's taverna on the beach.

'This way,' said Mal, taking Jane by the elbow. He had found what he'd known was out there.

Following the direction of the music they reached a small street which did not look in the least alluring. But experienced Mal knew that appearances in these cases were almost always deceiving. Unsavoury dives were his little speciality.

In contrast to the shadowy neighbourhood, the café was blindingly bright. They stood in the doorway, over which there was no sign, adjusting their vision to the interior. A waiter beckoned energetically and pointed to a table in the rear. No sooner were they seated than another waiter rushed at them with two rakis which he placed on the paper tablecloth and made enthusiastic gestures so they might understand that the drinks were gratis. They understood.

Mal knocked back his raki and asked for a bottle of retsina. Jane nursed her fire water, more interested in drinking in her surroundings. In the glare of striplights and some bare electric bulbs which hung from the fly-speckled ceiling, the mustard coloured walls looked slightly more yellow than brown. They were decorated only with a calendar advertising a restaurant in Suda and some aged posters of the Sumaria gorge. The doors, she noticed, were a good green. All the chairs and tables had been pushed against the walls to leave a large open space in the centre of the oblong room above which volumes of cigarette smoke eddied, dispersed and regrouped.

The band, consisting of bouzoukis, a lyre, a clarino, a violin, a guitar and some bagpipes played loud and frantic music, the sinuous high spirits of which made Jane think alternately of snakes, goats and the stylized waves she'd seen on vases in the Heraklion museum. At the end of the room, not far from their table, was the busy bar from which waiters ran to and fro with rakis and beers. She could spot no wine drinkers among the almost exclusively male clientele. Only a woman, alone at a table halfway to the door, had finished a bottle of rosé and was in the process of ordering another. Her obvious familiarity with the waiter marked her as one of the café's regulars.

The woman was smiling – a dreamy indulgent smile that lingered at the corners of her mouth long after the waiter had made his way to the bar, skirting the customers with deft, practised movements. It was a smile so sweet as to be nearly plaintive, coupled as it was with watery blue eyes ringed in royal blue with matching mascara, a thin face grown leathery from too many summers on the Mediterranean and hair which could no longer trust to holidays to maintain its original gold and so had been driven to desperate remedies. Her dress, made of that pleated cotton which Jane always regarded as the poor woman's Fortuny, was an aquamarine which clashed badly with the eye make-up. Plastic bangles of the same aquamarine decked toasted arms already braceleted by creased flesh. (Jane shuddered, resolved to switch her sun lotion from a twelve to a twenty.) She was long, dry and bony, as if the sun had sucked out all the moisture from the fruit of herself and left her a decorated hull.

'Look at that woman,' whispered Jane, but Mal did not hear her.

Then she realized that it was not the waiter who had inspired that mesmerized smile but the dancers. The dancers. They had taken a break and were now back on the floor and forming a long line, their arms raised up to their shoulders, their hands joined, linked together like the strings of lights along the port. The music began and they set off in a row, turning and twisting and doubling back on themselves as they covered the entire empty space in the middle of the café, stomping, jumping, leaning towards then away from each other. There were twelve of them. They were all men.

'That's the snake dance,' Mal informed her.

'The what?'

'Just watch.'

The dancers laughed and cried out and bared their teeth, some of which were beautiful, some of which were gold and some of which were rotten. Ages ranged from twenty to fifty. They wore old black trousers and jeans, scruffy T-shirts and heavy shoes which they used to augment the thud of their stomping. A few of them had knives thrust into their belts. There were several excellent moustaches. ('It's a gun culture,' Mal had explained as they'd passed another road sign that had been completely shot out. It was because of the war, of the Germans, he'd said with satisfaction. Cretans were fierce and brave.)

When they had executed a few turns the last dancer, the one at the end of the line, suddenly, as if at some secret signal, flipped his whole body over and kicked his heels in the air without letting go of the hand of his partner who looked as if, for a split second, he was supporting the other's entire weight. The audience clapped and cheered, the hero gave an exultant smile and the dancers continued on their endlessly weaving way.

Jane tried to imagine how she might describe their masculine hauteur in a travel piece: 'rough peacocks . . . unfettered male in all his archaic swagger . . . gender festivities in contemporary Crete . . . the Old Man is alive and well . . .'

'*Snake dance*,' Mal repeated and took her hand. She nodded and smiled. There was an excited colour in her cheeks which shone through her freckles and her tan.

'It's very old. No one knows how old.'

'Do you think it's related to the labyrinth and the minotaur and all that?'

'Possibly.'

'Look at that woman.' Jane leaned close to him so as not to be overheard, though there was slight danger of it with the band at fever pitch. But Jane was always careful about other people's feelings. It was one of the things Mal loved her for, one he thought might eventually serve as an example to himself who judged more quickly and harshly and could take perverse pleasure in the leap to conclusions. They speculated in whispers about the woman's nationality. Malcolm thought German. Jane said Swedish then switched to American. They decided that the dewy smile was fixed especially on the tallest dancer, a swarthy broad-shouldered man with a splendid moustache who, despite his size and his clumsy black boots, was surprisingly light on his feet. He was one of those with a knife in his belt. His hubris was impenetrable, and he betrayed no hint of any rapport with the besotted woman.

As was their habit, Malcolm and Jane quickly gave the pair nicknames. He was Boots and she was the Blue Woman.

Conversation was interrupted by a short fat man with a puffy face who tugged imploringly at Mal's sleeve. Mal flinched. He didn't like strangers touching him.

'Buy you drink,' the man offered, his speech slurred but looking harmless enough.

'Thanks but no thanks.'

'C'mon please, you Inglish I think.'

'No thank you, we're fine,' Mal said firmly though with an afterthought smile.

'I been Ingland. Is good. You look friend called Mick. Nice man. Nice woman.' He stared at Jane. 'I buy you drink.'

'Thank you,' answered Jane and was about to add, 'that would be lovely,' when Mal interrupted.

'Sorry. We're having a private conversation.'

'Why you not drink? Drink no good?'

'We like it very much,' put in Jane. 'And we like this place.'

'You don't like.' He leaned against Mal, his drink sloshing dangerously in his hand.

Their waiter appeared and escorted the man to his own table, smiling apologetically at his English customers.

'I come back Mick,' called the man, his boozy good humour restored.

'Not too soon, baboon,' Mal muttered then ordered another bottle of retsina and two rakis.

'I'm fine Mal,' said Jane gently.

'What's the matter?' He was suddenly petulant. 'Don't you like to go out? Don't you like to have fun? You wanted me to bring you here.'

'Of course. Of course I do.'

'One retsina and two rakis,' he ordered again. 'And don't talk to me that way in front of the waiter.'

'What way?' asked Jane, completely bewildered.

Mal didn't answer so she returned her attention to the woman. Again she traced the arc of her gaze to the tallest dancer. He wasn't handsome, having been cast in too coarse a mould, but his physique was impressive, and his magnetic field undeniably potent. Poor Blue Woman. Boots was indeed her image de l'amour.

'Am I boring you?' Mal suddenly asked.

Jane looked at him in amazement. The atmosphere between them had definitely soured. Of course drink did alter people's personalities, but was he becoming so regressive she'd better just say he never bored her? No, she quickly appraised. Still time to defuse him.

'Sorry,' she smiled, determined to keep it light and save

the evening. 'Can't keep my eyes off the Blue Woman. She fascinates me.'

'Is that why you wanted that little creep to join us?' he pressed, as if he hadn't heard her excuse.

The music stopped and the dancers dispersed to various tables where rounds of drinks awaited them. Jane and Mal watched to see if the Blue Woman would be joined by Boots, but he had vanished.

'Probably doesn't want his mates to see him with her,' said Mal, slurring his *s*'s. 'Probably picks her up later, screws her and goes home, wherever that is.'

'How do you know he screws her?' Jane felt indignant for the Blue Woman and, in consequence, rashly returned the conversation to work.

'Alison told me Justin's having a prostate operation.'

'I wouldn't believe anything Alison said – unless of course she has privileged information in this case. Anyway, why tell me now?'

'I just remembered. I thought it would interest you.'

'Well it doesn't.' Mal maintained his sulk.

'There are worse people to work for, you know.'

'He's a pillock.'

'Just because he scrapped your article – '

'You always side with the landlord,' he accused bitterly.

'That's unfair, Mal.' Jane struggled to remain rational. 'If it hadn't been for Justin, I wouldn't have got this freebie and we wouldn't be in Crete.'

'Have you ever gone out with him?'

What she saw in his eyes shocked her: a wave of paranoia cohesing, gathering force, cresting to break all over her. It was too late to advise him to stop drinking. Definitely too late.

'I know you Mick. We meet London.'

'Oh no,' groaned Jane. The fat man was back.

Mal didn't answer. The fat man bent closer.

'Remember? Costa!' He smacked his chest. 'Buy you drink.'

'Go away,' Mal enunciated and looked at Jane. 'He think's I'm *Irish*!'

'I been London. Is stupid place.' The fat man growled.

'Sometimes, yes,' Jane agreed as Mal kicked her under the table.

'Stupid people. Stupid place.'

'Stop leaning on me!' Mal raised his voice. Customers at adjoining tables stared.

Again the waiter intervened, this time directing the man to the green door. 'Mick,' he cried, 'Mick . . .'

'So long Pork Chop,' Mal smirked and ordered two more rakis.

'I don't want it,' Jane insisted, but no one paid any attention.

More customers had come into the café, and the waiters flew about like the lizards Jane and Mal had seen running over the walls of their rented villa. The music grew wilder. The dancers were even more intoxicated. One of them slipped and fell to the floor, but his partners, without missing a beat, yanked him laughing to his feet. The audience cheered. Not one of them was a tourist. The Blue Woman sipped her rosé with the same entranced expression. She looked as though she were about to float up to the ceiling and hover there like a figure in a Chagall painting. No one joined her, and, aside from the waiters, no one spoke to her. Nor did anyone stare at her or accost her. Clearly they were used to her. She was a familiar fixture whose presence was taken for granted.

Mal signalled for more rakis, even though Jane's remained untouched. It was when she turned to say no thank you that she realized she and the Blue Woman were now the only females in the place. She also saw the stack of rifles behind the bar.

The waiter brought the rakis and this time Jane drank hers. As she did so Malcolm filled her glass with retsina. It was nearly toppled when someone stumbled against the table. Pork Chop again.

'Please leave him alone,' pleaded Jane, but he took no notice. He seemed fixed on Mal the way the Blue Woman was fixed on Boots.

'Sorry Mick.'

'Piss off!' said Mal.

'I sorry. You sorry too Mick?'

Mal turned his back. Pork Chop moved to the other side of the table in order to look in his eyes.

'I say sorry, man.'

'Why don't you go boogie with the other yobs? Or won't they have you? Too fat and clumsy, huh? Too stunted.'

'What mean stunted?'

'It means small but imperfectly formed.'

'I no stunted, Mick, *you* stunted.'

Mal rose to his full six feet. Pork Chop continued to glare at him.

'Don't like you. Stupid Inglish. Woman nice. You stupid.'

Mal pushed him away hard, but he bounced back like a rubber beach toy. Everyone was watching. Mal seized his stained shirt front.

'Fuck off you little Greek git or I'll break your fucking jaw.'

'Dazzle him with irony,' drawled Jane.

For the third time the waiter attempted to rescue Mal and grabbed the fat man by the sleeve. But Mal maintained his grip on the shirt front. The waiter pulled. Mal hung on. Now Pork Chop looked worried. Jane was worried too.

Then the music stopped. At that exact moment the fat

man raised his voice and spewed a stream of Greek abuse at Mal. Apparently Pork Chop was a wit because everyone in the café screamed with laughter. Everyone except Mal and Jane and the Blue Woman who, also at that exact moment, tore her eyes from the dancers and looked at Malcolm and Jane. She looked at them as if she'd only just become aware of their presence, as if they came as a complete surprise to her, as if, for a split second, she really saw them.

Her mascara was melting in the heat, and her eyeliner and shadow had smeared calamitously, merging into two big circles so that she looked like a blue clown. Blue. The colour of the sea, the sea of love, of the Mediterranean that had seduced and dessicated her. What was her tragedy, Jane wondered in the midst of her own minor crisis. Where did she live and how? How did she get through the days waiting to be here – every night, here? Their eyes met. Then the woman assumed her smiling mask.

Jane blinked. That last raki was doing something strange to her vision. Loyally she placed her hand on Mal's arm, and the four of them stood like figures in a tableau vivant, two about to erupt, two attempting to prevent eruption, everyone else absorbed in the spectacle.

Once more Pork Chop shouted in Greek. Once more they all laughed. Mal was sweating, red in his face and red in his brain. He felt rage, mortification. Most of all he felt his own physical strength. His blow would have landed squarely on Pork Chop's jaw if another waiter had not joined the first and extricated him from Mal's grip, tearing the fat pest's shirt in the process.

'Mick,' he yelled as they dragged him away. 'I love you. I give you shirt. Take shirt. Take everything. I love you Mick.' Then something more in Greek.

The customers were ecstatic.

Jane looked to see where they were taking Pork Chop,

but the band started again and the dancers took to the floor, three more of them this time. She tried discreetly to make Mal sit down.

'It's all right now,' she soothed.

Mal jerked his arm away. 'You can stay if you want.'

'Why would I want?' she began, astonished, but Mal was already moving to the door. His progress was halted by the dancers who were weaving their way towards his side of the room. Boots was now last in the line. As he passed Malcolm he executed the twist, the jump and the kick, leaping higher than any of the others had done. He glanced round in cool triumph, and it seemed to Jane that his eyes briefly caught those of the Blue Woman who looked as if she might swoon. Jane thought of the guns.

She pushed her way through the applauding clientele, more of whom were arriving by the minute. Mal was already on the street when she caught up with him.

'You don't have to leave, you know,' he said, walking off.

'Of course I'm leaving. Why would I stay? How could I stay? I couldn't get home.' It was the wrong thing to say.

'You wouldn't have to come home.'

'Mal, that's crazy. I *want* to come home.' Why did she feel like crying?

'Suit yourself.' He was walking so fast now that she was half-running to keep pace with him.

'Are you all right?' she asked.

'Look, if you want to go back just say so.'

He was impenetrable. She tried to take his hand, she tried to tell him how perverse he was being, she tried to keep pace with him. But he had finished speaking for the time being, so they went on in silence. The streets were empty except for the cats. They'd wandered very far from the small parking lot where they'd left the car and probably would have spent hours searching were it not for Mal's wonderful sense of direction. Even so, the shadows, the echoes, the real or imagined footsteps, the unfamiliar territory and the pursuing image of stacked rifles meant their Budget rent-a-car could not appear soon enough. It was only when they were at last unlocking its doors that Jane remembered Mal was too drunk to drive.

All the way to the villa she clung to the strap of her seat belt, in spite of which she was hurled against the door whenever Mal took a corner at sixty. Glimpses of lovely familiar scenery flashed out of the night. She might never see it again, she thought. Yet she was unable to break Mal's implacable silence. For the sake of both their lives she decided to trust to his brilliant instincts and to the relative emptiness of the road. She stopped checking the speedometer. They approached the curve where the road swung sharply to the left and wound up a hill above a little bay. Lights in the taverna were still on. If only they could stop and sit somewhere quiet and safe. Just for a moment she thought of suggesting a drink, anything to make him stop driving, but already the taverna was out of sight. She must hang on to the end, her heart racing, her damp hands clenched. Barely slowing, Mal swerved into their dirt track, bumped violently towards the new white villas and pulled to a neat halt. He *was* a fantastic driver.

They sat in the dark, listening to their own breathing. Mal's came heavy and thick as it always did when he'd drunk too much. Jane's was quick and shallow. The lights in all but one of the apartments were out. It was their light. They'd forgotten as usual to turn it off. They felt trapped in the car, caught in the silence, each hoping and fearing that the other might speak. Jane knew for certain that Mal had not finished. He was letting the words rise slowly to the surface of his mind; they were gathering force, cresting to break all over her. Mal was picturing Jane's face in the café, happy and excited. She'd looked alive with curiosity and ready for anything.

'You'll end up just like her, you know.'

'Like who?'

'The Blue Woman.' He faced her. 'You'll sit in cafés, wrinkled and ridiculous and menopausal. Watching dark men. Hoping to catch one on a slow news night.'

'I don't find that a plausible scenario,' she sniffed. But the thought frightened her. Once, she felt sure, the Blue Woman, too, had been 'all shining.'

'You'll sit there like her, imagining you're still beautiful. It'll take more and more retsinas to make you believe your own fantasy. Especially when the time comes to go home alone. You'll be a sad case.'

'Oh that's so corny.' She was angry now. Then it struck her: they were having their first genuine row. And there was no stopping it. They had entered a war zone and must go on until one or the other surrendered.

'I know what you were doing back there.' Mal abruptly switched gear, arguing like he drove.

'Really? Well I certainly know what you're doing right here. You're trying to make me responsible for that farce in the café.'

'What farce?'

'Your massive sense of humour failure. Your losing your rag at that pathetic little man. Your irresponsible driving.'

'But I'm fine.' He held up his hands, as if to indicate that he was unarmed. 'Look at me. Do I look upset? It's you who's upset.'

'Is that surprising when you've just behaved like a lunatic? Over nothing?'

'I thought I behaved quite well considering the way you tried to make a fool of me.'

'Oh *I* see. I'm the Jezebel, I'm the traitor. I set it all up, laid a trap for you to fall in. I'm the villain and you're the victim.'

'You're awfully young to be so bitter.' Mal wore an expression of feigned concern. 'It's a shame.'

'Oh it's so cool now. If only it could have seen itself an hour ago . . .'

'Have you any idea how contorted your face is?'

'. . . defending its threatened masculinity, its precious pride . . .'

'Will you please not shout. People are trying to sleep.'

Mal had lured her into the argument then pretended to withdraw, leaving her alone with her conjured anger and nothing to confront. It was a sophisticated and original punishment for her equanimity. But she had no intention of allowing him to abandon her this way. She would drag him back into the fray. It shouldn't be that hard now she'd got going.

She was right. In no time at all they'd returned to Boots and Pork Chop and the Blue Woman, using them like chess pieces to advance their attacks. People whose names they didn't even know. People who were only stereotypes.

'Why are we fighting over a few Greeks?' exclaimed Mal in desperation. She had him now.

'You're a proper English xenophobe, aren't you.'

They exchanged abuses until a light went on inside the villa and shone directly on to the bonnet of the car.

'One of those sleepers you're so concerned about.'

'Now you've woken them. I hope you're satisfied.'

'Deeply! Perfectly!'

The light had broken the malign spell that held them. They felt both observed and absurd. Escaping the car, they switched the scene of their drama to their apartment where they went on trying to shout in whispers until the tears ran over Mal's face and he collapsed and cried in earnest. Unwillingly at first, then with increasing tenderness, Jane held him. She was resentful of the Blue fate he had predicted for her, no doubt as an act of retribution for some pain centred in his own past; a revenge for accumulated, if unintentional woundings. Blows not even delivered by herself but which he was returning by proxy. Yes, whatever has been suppressed must inevitably surface. And so she decided to believe this had all come about because he was unable to bear the thought of losing her, of their drifting apart, growing older. Hadn't he said as much many times? Wasn't that one of the reasons she liked him – his emotional vulnerability? Like everyone, he feared the future.

She failed to see how his tears came merely as the fitting climax to an exhausting evening. In the end sleep, the great referee, called a ceasefire and they lay down on their hard, narrow, single tourist beds.

In the morning Mal had forgotten most of what had happened after they left Xania. He gave no thought to the events in the café. For him the characters in that play were already ceasing to exist. He woke like a child, primed for danger and discovery and fun. But first there was Jane. She would be reluctant, he knew, with the shreds of last night still clinging to her. Why did she tolerate such clinging when life was so patently short? Besides, she preferred sex at night. She would be tired still and damp with negative emotion. He would burn her awake.

He flung his whole weight down beside her and she groaned and pulled the sheet over her head. Nothing a little extra enthusiasm would not cure, though, so he bit her nipples and pried her legs apart and went at her for the next twenty minutes, during which time she felt sure the bed would split beneath them. Malcolm was not slight.

Now she was awake and wondering how soon she might safely shift him off her without denting his elation.

'That's the way Alexander the Great made love,' he sighed, letting her breathe at last.

She hesitated before he spoke. Was he serious? 'Raki and sex must have addled your brains,' she started to say. Or perhaps 'I thought you read history' might be more appropriate. Then he smiled at her. His curls were tight with sweat. His eyes were all attention, hers alone. She returned his smile. She'd wait until after lunch to remind him that Alexander the Great was gay.

Strategy and Siege

DAMON GALGUT

They were stranger than most. In the course of his academic career – thirty years of papers, dissertations, opinions – he had encountered many people, some of whom had even become his friends. But in all human beings, particularly those he knew well, there was an element that felt odd to him and that seemed to merit his suspicion.

'People are strange,' he would say, as he got into bed at night.

'People aren't strange,' retorted Susan, flicking through the pages of *You* magazine. 'People are people. You can't understand them, is all.'

Susan was his wife. She had black hair and red nails. Her mouth was sulky and plump. There was an anger in her that seemed directed at him, for what he'd done, or had failed to do, to her. When she had left him the previous year for an overweight Israeli, his life had felt obscurely improved. She too – his wife – had been strange.

He was fifty-three. He had brown hair, cut short, with streaks of grey running through it. His beard, too, was silvering as he grew older. With his black-rimmed glasses, his colourless clothing, he was a figure he approved of in the mirror; he posed no threat to anybody. He was clearly, unequivocally neutral.

'You don't take action, David,' Susan told him when she left. 'You watch things, you don't participate. That's why you're an historian – it's all safely in the past.'

'History isn't *past*,' he cried, aggrieved, but later her judgement had pleased him. Theory was abstract and infinite, while action was finite and messy. Mess of any sort displeased him.

His life had been, for several decades now, relatively free of mess. Susan's departure had brought it back in. In a certain sense, then, none of it would ever have happened if it hadn't been for her. He would never have gone to Lesotho at all. More importantly, he would never have met the Mosterts.

The Mosterts, who were stranger than most.

Mrs Mostert – Sylvia – was a large, raw-boned woman with red hands and greying hair and a voice made hoarse with whisky. Despite her surname, she was Irish, and the lilt in her accent was almost obscenely anomalous.

It was she who had been there to meet him, at the edge of the rutted dirt road. He had followed the directions carefully. When he saw the house down the hill on the right, he had pulled over on the verge.

She was standing there, doing nothing, in a shapeless floral dress. She watched him with faded blue eyes.

'Am I in the right place?' he said timidly.

'Indeed you are,' she roared at him. She ignored his proffered hand and struck him hard on the back. She took his suitcase from him and walked ahead of him down the path.

'Here,' she said. 'I hope it suits.' The cottage was separate from the house. It was bare, almost spartan – a bed, table, chair – but he had stayed in worse. A watercolour hung on the wall.

'You take your meals with us up there,' she told him,

jerking a thumb at the main house. 'How long are you here?'

'About a week.'

'Lock the door when you go out,' she said. 'They steal.' After a pause, she explained: 'the kaffirs.'

He went with her to the house to meet the rest of her family. George Mostert stood up when he saw him. He was a little older than David. He was thin and very sad, with a black moustache shaped like a bow-tie. He was bald, but had combed his hair across his scalp. 'Pleased to meet you,' he pronounced, his voice trembling with suppressed tearfulness. He looked, and sounded, Afrikaans.

'This is Henrietta,' Mrs Mostert brayed.

He turned. Henrietta was there. She was perhaps nineteen years old. She was square and fat with placid eyelids and black hair piled on her head. Above her mouth there was the faintest, downy hint of a moustache.

'David Altman,' he told her.

'*Ja*,' she said. She looked bored.

The other player in the game was one he was never introduced to, but she came moving through the room at that moment: sinewy, lithe, her dark skin gleaming, she was in her early thirties, her figure inside her ragged maid's uniform the sleek, neat shape of a wasp's. She was carrying a tray with whisky glasses on top of it. She hesitated, not sure where to put it.

He knew her name, because Mrs Mostert said it then: 'Rose,' she said, 'on the piano, Rose. Where you usually put it,' she said.

Rose moved to the piano and put down the tray. She turned, wiping her hands on her apron. She had eyes as round as coins.

As she passed them and went out of the room, David happened to look back and he saw George Mostert's face:

a spasm passed across it, a pang of such acute longing that he seemed to be in physical pain.

Then he saw David watching and became expression-less again.

'Kaffirs,' said Mrs Mostert sadly.

He had found the advert in a magazine called *Travel and Fun*. Susan had subscribed to a variety of publications, which continued to arrive in his post-box long after she had gone. Most of them he consigned directly to the bin, but, bored one evening after work, he had paged listless-ly through this one.

There, in a corner on page 32, he read: VISIT FABULOUS LESOTHO, it said. SEE THABA BOSIU, 'MOUNTAIN OF THE NIGHT'. (There was a very bad hand-drawn mountain under-neath.) ACCOMMODATION: THE MOSTERT FAMILY. BED AND BOARD. A box number followed.

David had kept the magazine, he didn't know why exactly. But a few days later, on a sudden impulse, he had taken down a history of Lesotho from the books and jour-nals above his desk and turned to the chapter on Thaba Bosiu.

'It was here, in this natural stronghold, that the legend-ary King Moshoeshoe, founder of the Basotho nation, lived with his growing band of followers for forty-six years. In a time of darkness and upheaval – the *Difaqane* was in progress, banditry and cannibalism were rife – Thaba Bosiu withstood sieges by a host of marauding nations, from the Ngwane to the Boers to the British.'

He decided to write a paper on it. The history of Lesotho had of course been tirelessly dissected and analysed, but there was something about the mountain that compelled him. He had found a photograph of it in that first book he'd paged through. He sat for hours, gazing.

It was a monolith of earth, topped with a sandstone crown, which reminded him somehow of a tooth. Only one path led up to its summit; impregnable cliffs barred all other access. There was a supply of water on top. There was no need ever to come down if there was danger below.

'Look at it,' he cried. 'It was *built* to withstand a siege.'

He was speaking to a colleague at work, a tall bearded man called Lance.

Lance yawned. 'If that excites you,' he said.

He could not have said why, but its perfection did excite him; no soldiers or weapons could take it. It was only long after that he made a connection between Susan's departure and the obsessive fascination he felt: pain had besieged him like an army. He longed to protect himself from it.

He had arrived on Mrs Mostert's birthday. He only discovered this that night when he went into the house for supper and she handed him a conical hat with pictures of Santa Claus on it: 'I know it's a Christmas hat,' she cackled, 'but we have to look festive, don't we?'

She was turning fifty-seven. She sat at the head of the table, elbows planted on either side of her plate, bedecked in tawdry Christmas decorations. Mr Mostert sat next to David, a yoke of bells hung around his neck. His head was bowed with the weight of it, or shame.

Henrietta was opposite David. She sprawled in her chair, her flesh, her eyelids, indolent. She ate with lazy indifference, never quite closing her mouth, one hand all the while fiddling in her hair, winding and unwinding a coil around a fat finger. She looked blankly at him from her black, melted eyes in which the colour of the pupils had run. He thought she might have smiled at him once.

Sprigs of plastic mistletoe were stuck behind her ears.

He ate in appalled fascination. Mrs Mostert was the only one who spoke. Tossing back gulps of whisky with one fist, she held forth with stentorian fervour: 'We've been here six years now, David. In this hell-hole. We didn't buy this place – we inherited it. From my brother. He used to live here, don't ask me why. But we jumped at the chance to move here, 'cause we'd just lost our house up in Jo'burg. Him,' she cried accusingly, pointing with a half-chewed drumstick at her husband. Gobs of fat sprayed on the table. 'He lost everything!'

Mr Mostert smiled and sighed. 'Not *everything*, Sylvia,' he said.

'It's been hell here, David. A nothing country run by nothing people. I'd leave tomorrow, but you get trapped. I have my little guest cottage, *he*' – the chicken leg again – '*he's* got some new scheme going. And Henrietta's in her last year at school, of course, in Maseru. You can't just . . . uproot.'

'No,' said David, sweating. He felt he was stuck to his chair.

She asked him about his paper. He tried to explain, but could see immediately it was pointless. Her eyes were dulled with whisky and boredom. 'It's called *Strategy and Siege*,' he concluded lamely and sat hunched over his plate, while Henrietta picked at her teeth.

There were several courses to the meal, each one more tasteless than the last. None of them moved from their places. The plates were removed, and new ones brought in, by the black woman called Rose. She wore the same ragged maid's uniform from the afternoon and moved around the table in a monotonous orbit. As she bent over each place, her dark breasts lolled in their cloth; David's eyes were involuntarily drawn to George Mostert.

He had never seen a man so stricken. Whenever Rose came near him, his temples were basted in sweat. His skin took on a yellowish pallor and he gripped the edge of the table with his fingers, bending over his plate with such furious misery that it seemed amazing his wife didn't notice. The bells round his neck tinkled faintly.

But perhaps Mrs Mostert was not completely unaware. Certainly Rose occupied a central space in her attention: 'You can't get a good one. We've been through twenty maids. They lie, they steal, they cheat. *This* one's days are numbered.'

Or: 'She's everywhere, all the time, hanging around the house. They're obsessed with white people, you know.'

And later: 'It's a battle of wills, David. What goes on in the country is going on in the kitchen, I've always believed that's true.'

Through all of these and more acerbic asides, Rose moved with impervious calm. Mrs Mostert made no attempt to censor herself when Rose came into the room. Her bile mounted higher as the level of her whisky dropped. She spoke of darkies, of kaffirs, of 'them'. By the time dessert was served, it was evident to David that her invective was not directed at the nation of people whose country she unwillingly inhabited, but at the succession of faceless women who occupied her kitchen. Her hatred of Rose wasn't personal. But her hatred of her husband was.

At the conclusion of the meal, her family gave presents to Mrs Mostert. Two boxes wrapped in tinsel were placed on the table before her. 'Oh, look,' she cried, clapping her hands together. 'Look what they've done, David.'

He swallowed. 'I'm sorry,' he said, 'but I don't have anything to give you myself. I didn't know . . .'

'Of course you didn't, David. Don't worry.'

She was ripping out handfuls of tinsel.

George Mostert had given his wife a copper bracelet, but she barely glanced at this before tossing it aside. It was the other present that commanded her attention:

Henrietta had given her mother a box of chocolates. She held it up, a prize, her tiny eyes narrowed to slits.

'My baby,' she said to her daughter. 'Thank you, thank you, my baby.'

'OK,' said Henrietta vaguely. She was still twisting that thick strand of hair. Suddenly, without any warning, she looked directly at David. 'Are you going up there tomorrow?'

'I . . . Pardon?'

'Are you going up the mountain tomorrow?'

'I . . .' he said. 'Yes, I . . . I am.'

'Oh,' she said. 'I'll come with you.'

He stared at her, blinking.

'I'll come show you the way.'

The path was steep. It zigged back on itself halfway up. He had to stop and rest at this point, sitting on a rock. Henrietta came and sat next to him. 'Jissus, it's hot, hey,' she said.

He wiped his forehead with a hanky. It was only nine in the morning, but already the sky was brilliant with heat. He thought he saw a vulture, high up.

'It's hot,' he echoed vaguely.

Henrietta wore a cotton frock today and had a piece of ribbon tied in her hair. Despite the sharp stones, she carried her sandals in one hand and David had a vivid image of her feet, plump and splayed out on the rock. She was all flesh, Henrietta; ample, wanton, profuse.

She led him the rest of the way to the top. The crest of Thaba Bosiu was flat, covered in a skin of dry grass. Some of the original buildings were still standing, though the walls were sagging and collapsing. And there were mounds of stones heaped here and there, supposedly ready to repel invaders. He went to one of these piles.

'Be careful,' she told him, 'of snakes.'

So he moved hastily away. He was frightened of darkness and crevices, of what could emerge from small spaces. With his notebook gripped safely in one hand, his pen clenched between teeth, he strode out across the level plateau, stopping here and there to make notes.

There was not a lot to see. Congregated together at what seemed an arbitrary site, the graves of Moshoeshoe and some of his lesser descendants were grouped in a roughly rectangular formation. David paused there to pay homage, but they were also, in the end, stones. He tramped on. All was grass, termite hills, wind. He stumbled in a half-concealed furrow. He had read of a legendary red sand-dune which was blown around the hilltop by the wind, but which never left it; for all his searching, however, it remained concealed. Perhaps, after all, it had gone.

Henrietta had never heard of it. 'A sand-dune?' she shrilled, incredulous. 'There's no sand-dune up here!'

Her ribbon had come untied and those thick dark tresses had spilled down again; bovine, she lumbered beside him. The heat and effort made her sweat and her dress was pasted to her back.

He made a full circuit of the hilltop. It took two hours to do so. He made diagrams of various strategic points, but his concentration was muddled and splintered. Whenever he turned his head her round, ruddy face was floating. She batted her lashes at him. He could hear her open mouth breathing.

By the time he got back to where they had begun, he was dizzy with frustration and fury. He would have to return alone at some future point and redo all the work of that morning. A headache pressed the inside of his skull. His hands were trembling slightly. She plumped herself down on a rock like a huge and featherless fowl. She was monstrous. Leaving his notebook and pen on a stone, he withdrew behind some nearby aloes for an urgent release of his bladder. When he got back, she had doodled his name in the margin of a page and encircled it with inky blue flowers.

They went back down the hill together under that limpid, livid sky. It was too hot to work. He spent most of the afternoon undressed on his bed, thrashing in racked semi-sleep. The shutters threw shadows on him. What would Susan have said to this? He, the observer, who had spent so much of his life in rational thought, had detected something in himself that felt suspiciously irrational. The historian was obsessed by the future.

He woke at twilight, his mind clear and lucid. He could leave. There was nothing to force him to stay.

When Mrs Mostert hammered on his door shortly afterward, he told her he didn't want any supper. 'I have a fever,' he said. 'The heat.'

'Shame,' she said, sceptical. 'I'll send Rose down with medicine.'

He waited. When the light in the dining-room went off and the one in Mrs Mostert's bedroom came on, he was ready. He had packed up his bag. He had left a note, claiming 'personal matters', and a week's rent on his pillow. He slipped out, closing the door softly behind him. Feeling as febrile as he had claimed to be, he moved around the side of the house to the path that led up to his car. As he passed the lounge window he stopped, as rigid as if he'd been called.

Henrietta was slouched in the armchair near the window, wearing a voluminous white gown. Her hair was unpinned, spilling down like oil on her shoulders as her arm moved sluggishly up and down, engaged in some robotic activity. Then he saw: she had on her lap the box of chocolates she had given to her mother last night. Mindlessly, stupidly, she was unwrapping chocolates, then conveying them up to her mouth. Her jowls worked thickly as she chewed.

He was anguished. He stood there, horrified, transfixed. He started to sweat copiously again.

She took a last chocolate, then closed the box. He watched her unblinking as – a cow heaving out of the grass – she got to her feet. She stowed the box in the sideboard, where her mother had put it, and stood there another moment, sucking indolently on her fingers.

How her fat lips could suck.

He gave a small, throttled cry. His glasses tilted sideways on his nose as he blundered blindly away. As he staggered down across the prickling lawn, through a darkness threaded with fireflies, he heard a hiss of breath from the shadows on one side.

It was George Mostert, lurking near the hydrangeas. He was smoking a cigarette, the tip of which glowed red, another firefly. He seized David by the arm. 'Come,' he said. 'I want to show you something.'

He took him to the bottom of the garden. There, in a stack of wire-fronted hutches, piled in rows on top of each other, were rabbits: shaggy as goats, they flopped and tumbled under mesh. David caught a glimpse of eyeballs and flat, wedge-shaped ears. An unpleasant odour wafted out.

'Angoras,' explained Mr Mostert feverishly. 'She mocks me, but this scheme will *work*. Do you have any idea what one pelt is worth? Do you know how quickly they breed?' He had rounded on David as if expecting replies, but abruptly he lowered his tone. He whispered: 'I saw you see.'

He felt sick. 'What?'

'I saw you see me. *Looking*.' He had hold of David's upper arm again. 'I can't help it,' he said. 'I want her. But *she, she* keeps watching. She won't let it happen. Because it's happened too often before. Do you know what it feels like to be watched?'

'No,' David said.

'Do you think I can have her?'

'Oh, God,' David pulled free. 'I don't know, I don't know what's happening.'

It was only now that Mr Mostert noticed his suitcase. He stared at it in surprise. 'Where are you going?'

'Nowhere,' David said. 'I'm not going anywhere.'

'It's her,' Mrs Mostert said. 'Of course it's her.'

She was sitting in the lounge, the opened box of chocolates on her lap. Her face was mottled with fury.

It was the next day. David had come in for lunch. Mrs Mostert held out the box to show him.

'Look at this, David. What did I tell you?'

He stood there, speechless, amazed.

'Well,' she said. 'That's it. She must go.' She stood up. 'I'll go and do it now.'

It was accomplished quickly. Mrs Mostert fired Rose in less than two minutes, her lilting voice droning out of the kitchen into the dining-room, where they all three sat in stupefied silence around the table. Nobody moved. David looked at George Mostert. He was bowed over, his face drained and haggard, his sad moustache twitching as he breathed.

Then he looked at Henrietta. She had her chin cupped in one hand and she was gazing obliquely at the ceiling. She seemed distant, preoccupied, as if her mind were on other, more important things.

A fly sawed lazily somewhere.

He had an urge to speak, but he didn't know what to say. *I watched you? I know it was you?* Under the table, Henrietta's knees were pressed lightly, insistently, against his. They felt as hot as two suns.

Mrs Mostert returned. She was flushed with the rapture of victory. She sat in her place at the head of the table, her massive bulk dispelling the air.

'That's done,' she said. Her voice had the resonant timbre of satisfaction in it. She reached for her whisky glass. 'I told her she can go in the morning.'

David saw Rose later that same day, when she passed him on the lawn on the way down to the compost heap. She was carrying a bucket of slops. There was nothing in her face or the way that she walked that registered what had happened to her that morning. She was inscrutable.

He waited for her to come back. He wanted to say something to her, but when she did return along the little path, humming lightly to herself, words failed him; he leaned weakly against the bole of a tree. She cast a curious glance as she passed him.

His paper was ruined. He knew he could never write it now. His inspiration had been destroyed by that slattern-ly girl with her faint hint of a moustache. He felt himself the centre of some devious design, the full extent of which was not apparent to him. She was everywhere. When he wandered on to the lawn outside, she would be casually loitering under a tree. When he tried to take a stroll up the road, he would catch a glimpse of her squatting lump-ishly on a stone. Always she would be twisting that same coil of hair, as if winding him in on a reel. Her heavy-lidded eyes were rolled towards him in their bed of edible flesh.

He shuddered. This was absurd. He determined to make a last effort to reimpose order upon this chaos. He sat down in his room at his little desk, with his few pages of notes spread out before him. He held his pen poised in one hand. He cleared his mind in preparation.

There, in the margin, was his name, with its corona of encircling flowers.

He burst into tears. He sobbed passionately for several minutes, banging his forehead on the desk. He hadn't cried in three or four decades and it occurred to him Susan would be proud. When he had composed himself again, he ventured out into the garden. Mrs Mostert was bent over a complex bush, wreaking havoc with her shears. She straightened up as he approached, glaring from under her sun-hat.

'Sylvia,' he said. 'I have to talk to you.'

'Yes?' She had smears of mud on her forehead.

'The chocolates. It was Henrietta. I saw her.' He explained.

She listened without expression. When he had finished, she wiped her chin with the back of one hand. 'I know,' she said.

' . . . Pardon . . . ?'

'I know. Henrietta loves chocolates. That's why she gave them to me.'

'But I don't understand. Why . . .'

She sighed. 'If it wasn't the chocolates, it would be something else. I don't keep maids very long. You can't trust them. These aren't white people, David.'

'But Rose . . .'

Mrs Mostert shrugged hugely. She cast a glance across the lawn at the scrawny figure of her husband. 'I never did like her,' she said.

That evening, after he had sat down at the supper table, David said: 'I think I'll be leaving in the morning."

They looked at him. He was accused by their eyes.

'I . . . I've done my research,' he stuttered. 'There's nothing to keep me here now.'

He had spent three hours working up to this announcement and had anticipated an immediate sense of relief. But instead his oppression was greater. He felt that he had failed each of them in some crucial, some cardinal way.

The cruellest trial of all was to endure those eyes, beneath their purplish, sybaritic lids.

'This mutton is excellent,' he whispered, to placate her.

But Mrs Mostert only grunted disdainfully.

It was the worst meal of his life. There was a leaden silence in the room, broken by the dashing of spoons and the bestial grinding of teeth. At some point in the evening the electricity gave out and they proceeded in thickening darkness. A storm was coming up outside. The curtains billowed in on hot gusts of wind and distant lightning guttered on their faces.

To make matters worse, Rose was waiting on them. Shadowy, wordless, she passed in and out of the room, bearing trays, carrying plates. He tried to see her face, but it was too dark. Nevertheless, he had the growing suspicion that some coded communication was taking place. It seemed to him that, as she dished up the food, Rose lingered by George Mostert's place. And once, in a particularly fitful burst of lightning, he thought he glimpsed her arm pressing unnaturally close to Mr Mostert's. In the silences between thunder, he could hear the wheezing breath of the man on his right and detected the high note of anguish.

But his curiosity was soon quelled, because something similar was happening to him. As she reached for her glass of water, the edge of Henrietta's hand brushed his. He withdrew sharply, but a minute later her bare foot rubbed at his ankle. He sat still, suppressing his cries.

It was fitting, somehow, that these signals should be sent through the dark in the baleful presence of the woman.

When the last course had been concluded, George Mostert said distinctly: 'I'm going to see to the rabbits.'

Rose was standing in the shadows. David saw her look up.

Mrs Mostert said, 'I don't care where you go, George.'

But he repeated slowly: 'To the rabbits.'

David fled, reeling, to his room. He had the conviction that something was about to happen. The light was off here too. He crouched on his bed, lifting up the edge of the curtain to look out. He saw George Mostert go past, leaning into the wind. He waited a few minutes. Then Rose also came by, looking carefully behind her. She vanished down the path in the darkness.

Then he knew that his turn was coming. He was filled with a gassy euphoria which gave way, in a moment, to terror. He became desperate and flailed about frantically, searching for a key with which to lock the door, but there was none. So he pushed the desk against it. He undressed and got into bed. He discovered he was trembling violently and tried to calm himself by counting, but the numbers wouldn't follow in sequence. So he tried to pray, but the words petered out. Then he simply lay there. Waiting.

'*Dawid*?'

She said his name in Afrikaans. This seemed in itself an outrage. Raising himself on his elbows, he could see her florid face wedged in the crack of the half-open door. With a heave she shoved it wide, sending the desk skidding backwards. She came in and closed the door behind her. She had on the voluminous white robe that he'd seen her in last night. She padded to the bed and loomed over him, massive as a monument.

'Move over,' she whispered.

He did. Now that she was here – where she should never have been, in tactile, assailable proximity – she wasn't nearly as vast or powerful as his mutinous mind had made her. She pulled back the sheets and got in. She lay passively, waiting for him.

The terror and panic had subsided and he was lucidly, even coldly, calm. It became apparent to him that he had made a mistake. The allusions and little physical contacts that had rocked his psyche like a rowing-boat now seemed pointless, a ridiculous game. It was absurd that he should be here, in this compromising moral position. He was a respected academic with a reputation for formality and correctness. She was an overweight farm girl with some kind of hormonal problem. His duty revealed itself to him.

He cleared his throat. 'Uh, Henrietta,' he said. 'I think . . . we should . . . reconsider.'

She didn't seem to have heard him. She took his hand and placed it over her breast.

'No,' he said. 'Henrietta. No.'

He withdrew his hand. She became enraged. She sat up squarely in the bed.

'What's the matter?' she yowled. 'What's the matter?'

She got up and went out. She slammed the door loudly behind her. He lay in the bed, a vast relief spreading from him. He had done the right thing in the end.

A minute later, it occurred to him that perhaps he had, after all, been wrong. The indentation in the bed next to him was still warm. In his mind he saw again her hair, the pout of her lips. He felt rocked by a terrible pain. He got out of bed quickly and floundered to the door and out, banging his head on the lintel. He hissed her name into the wind and darkness, peering for a glimpse of her white robe. But she was gone. The other house was dark.

He felt breathless, demented. The mad passions had risen in him again and he felt capable of some extreme deed, if he could only think of one. He wandered in a daze halfway down the slope and then stopped there, bent over, to catch his breath. The first drops of rain were falling.

He was still there, crouched over in that position, when Rose passed him on her way up from the rabbits. As if this was a normal sight – a middle-aged man in his underwear, standing wheezing in a storm – she nodded at him as she went by.

'Hello,' he whispered hoarsely.

A few minutes later, George Mostert followed. He had a strange expression on his face. His jersey was on the wrong way round and there were leaves and burrs on his clothes. He didn't say anything to David, but as he trotted by in the gloom he smiled cryptically, significantly, at him. He passed him and went up to the house.

In the morning, the fragmented world of last night began, once again, to cohere. It had rained heavily and steam was rising from the ground. There was a sense of re-newal: birds called piercingly from the trees, the leaves seemed heavy with sap. He packed his suitcase for the second time since he'd arrived and went out into the sunlight.

George Mostert was the only one who came out to say goodbye. His wife, he explained, had gone shopping. He was shaved and looked rested. The two men were cordial with each other.

'Have a safe trip,' Mr Mostert said.

'Good luck with your rabbits,' said David.

They shook hands. Then David was walking back up through the trees, to where his car was parked. He stopped once and looked back, but the house was cloistered and dark.

As he loaded up his suitcase and started the engine, he felt happy enough to whistle. He went so far as to hum as he drove slowly down the track.

About half a kilometre down, still a little way from the tar, he came to a figure at the side of the road. It was Rose.

She was walking slowly but doggedly, weighed down with a suitcase twice as large as his. He stopped for her. She got into the seat next to him, sitting composed, her hands clasped together in her lap.

'Where to?' he asked.

But she didn't answer. He understood that she was travelling his way. They drove in companionable silence down the narrow stripe of dirt, the mountain receding behind them.

After they had reached the tar and gone on a short distance west, another car approached, going in the opposite direction. As it passed, he saw that it was driven by Sylvia Mostert, the back seat piled up with parcels. She saw him and then she saw Rose. Her face was momentarily transfigured with shock.

The two cars went past each other.

A little way further, Rose said to him: 'Here.'

It was the only word he ever heard her speak.

'Here?'

It was a featureless expanse of plain, the earth extending in gradations of deepening colour towards a distant, blue line of mountains. She got out and he helped her unload her suitcase. They stood there another moment, awkwardly.

'Well,' he said. 'Goodbye.'

She smiled at him sweetly, her face imperturbable, unworried. Then she picked up her suitcase. The last sight he had was of her departing back as she toiled away slowly into the landscape. He started to get into the car, but changed his mind. Instead he stayed where he was, leaning on the roof, watching her grow smaller and smaller. Eventually she sank into distance and he couldn't see her any more. But in all the time that it took her to vanish, she never once looked back.

Strangeness and Charm

STEVEN KELLY

Grace liked to model nude as much for the money as for the pleasure of being admired by the artist she was working with. She made them pay double the usual rate if they wanted her nude. Call it danger money she would tell them. If I wear no clothes I don't know what else you might want or I might catch a chill. If she did not trust them she would ask for cash up front. New clients would complain that they were poor and some even thought that the extra money they paid gave them the right to touch her or to peer closely between her legs. That's enough of that, she would say. Paint! Draw! Sculpt! Get to work. My time is your money.

The money came in useful. If she modelled nude she could buy herself perfume or clothes from the boutiques. Otherwise she could not afford nice things and the nice things themselves were an investment of sorts. If she dressed well and wore Chanel or Dior she could be sure of a good meal most nights of the week, and gifts of course. Always gifts. Only the other day Angel had given her a beautiful pendant, the silver cross studded with sapphires which she was wearing while she modelled for him now.

'If you just move your . . . yes, just draw it . . . yes, that's it.'

Angel had been one of her regulars for years. He was in

love with her as most of her regular clients were in one way or another. The photographer, Claudia, loved her for her full lips and for the way her face could look like another person's with only the slightest change of the light or her make-up. Henry, the crazy Englishman, he loved her for the way she smiled at him after their sessions together. At least that was what he had said once. Gianni was more brutal. Your tits are the best, he would say. Every time she worked with him. Your tits are the best and you've got a decent pair of legs. It counts for something. And Angel? He had just murmured it in her ear one night at an opening of his work: I love you. Almost as if he were trying the words out. He had never mentioned the evening again.

Angel. Her longest standing client by far. Usually even the artists who liked her best grew tired of painting the same face, the same figure so many times and they would move on to someone else, someone not better, but different. Angel kept asking her back. She did not know what he saw in her, what it was about her that he loved. Not her lips or face or her smile or her tits or legs, she was sure of that. Did he even desire her? She could not say.

'And now cock your . . . As you were . . . yes.'

Certainly, whatever he felt or thought, he always behaved like a perfect gentleman. He had not tried to touch her, did not even look at her if they were taking a break or while she was undressing or dressing which was strange because most of her clients liked to watch her undress or dress even if they pretended to look the other way. The very fact of his inscrutability in this made Grace uneasy. The opaqueness of his look and her own vanity conspired, indeed, to fascinate her.

'Let's take a . . . Would you like . . . No, no, you relax, I'll . . .'

She watched him as he crossed to the small kitchen unit in the corner of the studio and filled the kettle. She was tempted to ask him. What do you want from me, Angel. Why am I here. Tempted to ask, but she bit her tongue. There was the money to think of. She stood up and threw a shawl around her shoulders and walked over to stand beside him. He glanced at her a little nervously and she smiled.

'Angel, could I have coffee? I know I don't usually but for a change I think I should like some. With sugar. *Macchiato.*'

He switched off the kettle and unscrewed the espresso machine and filled it with water and coffee grounds.

'Coffee, yes. Sugar, two? Three? Milk, coffee, yes . . .'

She giggled and he turned to look at her again, frowning.

'Nothing, Angel, it's nothing. And how is the painting? Will it be long now? No, no, as long as you need. I just wondered.'

She walked back to the easel and stared at the canvas for a while until Angel cleared his throat behind her and handed her the cup of coffee.

'Do you . . . I mean . . . is it . . .'

She took the coffee and looked again at the painting.

'It's perfectly wonderful, Angel. You've caught the light just so and your line is excellent. And it's quite beautiful.'

And really it was beautiful. It took her by surprise. Angel was a technician, all the critics said so. A very good technician, to be sure, but what they meant when they said so was that Angel's paintings lacked soul, that he gave nothing of himself to his work.

'What will you call it?'

'I thought . . . if you don't mind . . . perhaps . . . *Grace.*'

Grace was quiet for a moment and looked carefully at the face on the canvas. Normally she found it hard to

associate herself with what she was made into by the
artists she worked with and often, even if the artist or
someone else commented on the likeness, she herself
could barely see any resemblance. She nodded and turned
and kissed Angel lightly on the cheek before he had a
chance to shy away.

'Yes, you must call it *Grace*. I am Grace and this is me.
And you're an angel. Of course.'

When she had drunk her coffee Grace threw off her shawl
and took her place on the banquette. Yes, Angel fascinated her despite herself. He was so strange at times, so
unexpected. This pendant for example. She liked it very
much and it suited her but it was not the sort of thing
she would have expected as a gift from him. He had given
her things before, many things. A new coffee maker for
her birthday, a dress one time when he wanted to take
her to a ball and she said she had nothing to wear.
Versace. Quite stunning and very expensive. He had paid
her telephone bill once when she had no money and
was sued by the telephone company and even gave her
a new television set which had remote control, because
she was so lazy, he said. But he had never given her anything which had no purpose, no use in the way that
this silver cross had no use unless it were simply to flatter
her *décolletage* if that were a use, or to ward off demons if
there were such a thing or he believed that there were. You
must wear it for me always, he had said. Wear it every
time you model for me. For luck, he said. Perhaps he did
see himself as a demon. Or perhaps he did desire her and
his desire was his demon, something from which he
sought to shield her, and himself, through his gift. Grace
smiled.

'Are you . . .'

'Why no, I am sorry. I was dreaming, letting my

imagination run away with itself. It's nothing, I'm fine. Continue.'

She took up her pose again and let her gaze wander from Angel's face to his hands to his legs and back up the length of his body again. He was not unattractive. Not unattractive at all. He was tall and quite elegant and if his chin was weak and his midriff starting to fill out at least his shoulders were broad and his legs long and slim. She tried to imagine him without clothes. Tried to imagine the tone of his flesh, to think how his veins might look beneath his skin. His muscles and tendons. It was difficult. She had never seen him except fully clothed, usually wearing his tweed jacket or with a shirt and tie under his smock as he was now. She had only his face and hands to go on and together they were a paradox for his face was quite chubby, the skin sallow, whereas his hands were bony, sinewy, calloused. She could not guess what the rest of him might look like. Unable to help herself she yawned.

'Oh, but you're . . . We must . . .'

'But no, Angel, I'm not at all. Really, and it's not as if I have to do anything. Please carry on.'

'No, no, I insist . . . We can . . . Tomorrow. There's always . . .'

Grace allowed him to have his way and started to dress.

'You're so very sweet, Angel. At what time shall I come? In the afternoon would be better for me. You know how I am before lunch. And remember that I don't even get out of bed for less than ten thousand lire.'

'Perhaps . . . I mean . . . We could . . . Would you . . .'

Grace smiled and pretended to think: 'Very well, but not French tonight, Angel. Let's have something different for a change. Spanish perhaps or even Italian if that doesn't bore you. Pick me up at nine.'

*

When she got back to her apartment she slept for a while. Then she bathed and made herself up more carefully than usual. She wore an off-the-shoulder red dress and sheer stockings and high heels and stood in front of the mirror, practising her smile and posing in as languid a fashion as she could, hips and one shoulder thrust forward, an imaginary cigarette in hand. When she was happy with the way she looked she opened some wine and poured herself a glass and put on some music and waited for Angel to arrive. Just as the doorbell rang she realized that she had forgotten to wear the silver cross Angel had given her and she hurriedly fastened it around her neck as she went to let him in.

'Shall we . . . Or would you . . .'

'No, Angel, I've just opened a bottle of wine. It's quite good wine from the Adige so come in and then we will go. When is the table booked for? Nine thirty? That's OK, they know you there, surely. They'll hold it for us. You don't need to have wine. There's beer, of course, and some vodka somewhere, in the freezer I think. Russian. Just help yourself.'

Angel took a glass of wine and looked around her apartment as if he had never seen it before. Grace sat down and motioned to him to take a seat which he did.

'Yes, did you notice it? He's a pornographer, really, and not nearly so good as you. Still, it brightens the place up and it was kind of him. He was offered a lot for it by some rich woman who buys his stuff all the time. When he tires of me I shall sell it to her. Unless she tires of him first of course.'

'But I'm . . . I mean . . .'

'Oh, they all tire of their models eventually, Angel. You know that quite as well as I do. All of them apart from you. You're a rock in my life. You're an angel.'

*

At the restaurant Grace said that she would have whatever Angel liked to choose. He ordered in Spanish, fish and salad. And they drank sangria and ate olives.

'Do you . . . I mean . . . Is it . . .'

'But I adore it. Chin chin.'

She raised her glass and Angel did the same. His eyes kept flicking to the silver cross around her neck and Grace could not help herself. She held the cross up, presented it to him. 'Back, Satan,' she said. She giggled and Angel blushed.

'But I . . . I'm . . . I was . . . I mean . . .'

Grace giggled again and, dropping the cross, took hold of his hand.

'No, I'm sorry, Angel. I should not laugh at you now. And it is so beautiful. You must look. And didn't I promise you that I would wear it for you always? I did and I am, so of course you must. It's not your fault. It's just the way pendants are made. Or the way women are made, at least.'

'I . . .'

'Do you know, working today has tired me out. You would never think it, would you, that lying on your back all day could be so tiring. And if you don't believe me you should try it. Really, one day I shall make you, I shall take your place and you can take mine. I will paint you, and you can lie still all day and see how it feels. Oh, but I'm not complaining, just saying.'

As usual Angel had little to say while he ate which suited Grace because his lack of humour had oppressed her mood. Occasionally her eyes were drawn to his hands, to the precision with which he used his knife and fork to separate flesh from bones, the almost dainty way he transported his food from plate to mouth. It was part of his problem, she decided. He was so conscious of being on display that his concern for appearances paralysed him. Struck him dumb. It did not irritate her in itself so much as the fact that his fastidiousness made him even more of a mystery to her. She could find nothing behind his mannerisms in the same way that she could find no clue behind the mannered style of his painting as to what really drove him, what made him tick. What do you want from me Angel, she muttered to herself. What is it you want.

'I'm sorry . . . did you . . . Oh.'

Grace sighed: 'Sometimes I cannot eat. It is as if I have no energy for it. Do you ever feel that?'

Angel frowned and waved a hand helplessly and said nothing. Again Grace saw how his gaze drifted to the silver cross. He did not even seem to notice that he was staring at her like this, so boldly. It irritated her. Such a contrast to the way he respected her in the studio when she was naked and he was painting and could barely allow his eyes to rest on her body for more than a few seconds. She slapped the table top: 'But enough, Angel!'

He flushed and mumbled something and excused himself to go to the bathroom and Grace lit one of the slim cigars she sometimes smoked after eating in the evening. She felt ruffled and needed to compose herself. She played with the pendant, running her fingernail across the gems set in the silver. It was very old of course, and must have been expensive. And it was beautiful, but suddenly she disliked it. She disliked it for what it represented, not to her but, as it seemed, to Angel. A charm, he had called it when he gave it to her. She had thought the word strange but not unusual for Angel who often used words which she would not. I have bought this small charm and I should like you to have it, he had said. A charm, something to protect her, keep her safe, but ironically something which drew attention to her vulnerability as much as it advertised her virtue.

Angel returned and took his seat.

'I have asked for the bill. We should go now, Angel. We can have coffee at your place, or mine.'

At his apartment, above his studio, Angel made coffee while Grace looked for some music.

'Blues, blues and more blues,' she shouted to him. Finally she gave up looking and sat on the floor in front of the empty fireplace and Angel joined her a few moments later.

'You have none of your own paintings here. It's strange. As if you want to hide from your work. Is that how it is? I suppose you need only go down the stairs and it is there, of course. But still, you paint your pictures and then do not have them to enjoy in your own home. Perhaps it would seem like vanity to you.'

Angel reached over to her and stroked her shoulder with the back of his hand. Grace shook her head: 'No no no. You cannot do this. Tell me, when you paint what do you think of? I'm curious because when I model for you I think of all sorts of things because of course I have nothing else to do, but you, what do you think of? Do you have to think in order to paint? Or does it come naturally, does it come without thought? Tell me, I should like to know.'

Angel said nothing, did not even seem to hear her. He stared at the cross around her neck, leaned towards her so she could feel his breath on her cheek. She moved away.

'Please, Angel. Here, I shall take it off, your cross. I mean, it cannot be my perfume which is making you crazy like this.'

Again he reached out, now grazing her neck and cheek with a fingernail. Grace took his wrist in one hand and held the cross in the other.

'Angel, do not do this. It is not what I want. It is not what you want either. You'll see. When you wake up in

the morning you shall realize that this is not what you
want. Please, stop now. That is all.'

He frowned and drew his hand back, his eyes still fixed
on the cross which Grace was holding now between her
thumb and finger.

'I . . .'

'Do you know, I should like to view your painting.
Grace. Can we go down and see it? I know it isn't finished
but still, I should like to look at it now.'

Angel shrugged and Grace took his hand and led him
out of the apartment and down to his studio.

She was almost surprised to see the canvas still on its
easel. It seemed somehow improper to her that it should
be there, in full view of the room, as if it were she who
were on display for anyone to see if they should walk in.
Angel had become morose and instead of looking at the
painting with her, he took off his jacket, loosened his tie
and sat down on the banquette by the window where she
usually posed for him. Grace pulled up a stool and sat in
front of the painting, staring at it intently. Yes, he had
caught the light just so, his line was excellent, it was
beautiful. And it had soul. It had, somewhere, something
of Angel in it. She searched the canvas. Not the Angel she
knew from days and weeks and years of modelling for
him, of dinners and parties and openings, but yes, something of the downcast, forlorn Angel who was falling
asleep on the banquette in front of her now. Grace touched
the pendant. Of course he had not bought it as he had
said. It must have been his in the first place, she was sure.
A family heirloom or a gift from an old lover or what did
she know. A charm. In any case this cross was significant
to him, had some meaning to him which could draw out
his desire. And it was his desire which he had put into his
painting, it was his desire which had unmasked him.

'You do not love me.'

'I . . . But . . .'

'It does not matter, but I like to know. To know where I stand.'

And she did know where she stood. She was a model to him and nothing more. Someone he could pay to model nude for him, someone he could even admire for her beauty. But more than anything someone he could clothe in the associations of his own mind.

'Angel, will you take me home?'

At her apartment Grace stayed up until late into the night drinking iced vodka and toying with Angel's charm. She held it tightly so the sapphires and the sharp silver corners bit into her, leaving their imprint on her skin.

Sukie

FRANCIS KING

After the lecture, the dean of the medical school said: 'Maybe you are hungry. Maybe I should take you somewhere out to dinner.'

The apparent half-heartedness of the invitation must, Middleton decided, be due to the fact that, though the Korean had spent a year at Guy's, he still had a shaky grasp of English.

'It's very kind of you. But I think I'll take myself off to an early bed. I still haven't got over my jet lag.'

The dean at once relaxed, he even smiled. His relief was unflatteringly obvious. 'Yes. Yes, I understand, Dr Middleton.' No doubt, Middleton thought, his one wish was to be rid of this dreary old buffer foisted on to him by the British Council. 'Then I will call the car for you.'

'Oh, no need for that! I can easily walk.'

'No, no, Dr Middleton!' The dean sounded shocked. 'You must not walk.'

'The hotel's so near.'

'It is late. You are tired. I will call the car. The driver is waiting for you. University driver,' he added. 'It is his job. He is paid to drive guests.'

As Middleton was about to dive into the back of the cumbersome, black saloon, the door of which the driver was holding open, the dean gave a deep bow. 'We are very grateful,' he said. 'That was quite an interesting lecture.

Our students learned much.' *Quite* an interesting lecture?
Then Middleton reminded himself that foreigners tended
to be confused about when 'quite' qualified praise and
when it intensified it.

Middleton's first thought was to go straight to bed. But
then an embarrassing rumble of his stomach just as he
was leaning forward to take his key from the desk clerk,
reminded him that he ought to eat. Perhaps he would try
the Café Good Luck, which he could see at the far end of
a foyer crowded with the suitcases of a party of French
tourists. These tourists had kept him from approaching
the desk for several minutes, as they had elbowed each
other, filled in their reservation cards and then, in many
cases, argued about the rooms allotted to them.

The head waiter's English was far superior to the
dean's. He was also far more welcoming. Having bowed
repeatedly to Middleton, the sleek back of his head reflect-
ing the light above him, he had asked: 'Alone, sir?'

'Yes, alone. I'm afraid so. All, all alone.'

'No problem.' He smiled and extended a hand in invitation. 'Please, sir.' As he led Middleton through a long,
cavernous room, he would from time to time swivel his
head, flash a smile and, with a strange bobbing motion of
his body, almost a bow, repeat: 'Please, sir. This way, sir.
Please.'

The room was full of unoccupied tables, laid with glistening white cloths, glittering cutlery, and vases with arti-
ficial flowers sticking out of them like feather dusters.
Why could he not sit at one of these tables? Middleton
wondered.

Now they were passing a horseshoe-shaped counter, at
which half a dozen or so people were seated. Then they
moved into an area behind it, invisible to anyone at a table
in the main room.

Here, in contrast to the main room, hardly a table was

empty. There were a surprisingly large number of women either alone or in pairs, each with a cup of coffee or a glass of Coca-Cola or orange juice in front of her, and there were some couples, male and female. The women were, almost without exception, young, elegant, attractive. Middleton guessed that the men, mostly middle-aged or elderly and wearing sombre dark blue or dark grey suits with ties no less sombre, must be drawn from the Japanese business-men who made up a major part of the hotel's clientele.

'This OK for you, sir?' the head waiter asked, yet again bowing and yet again flashing his brilliant, vacant smile.

'Fine, thank you.'

On Middleton's right were two attractive young women; on his left a far less attractive older one, in thick glasses with huge, diamanté-encrusted frames, which glittered in the light from the chandelier above her as she turned her head to look him over. A moment later, the two attractive young women also turned their heads. One of them smiled at him. Then she leaned across the table to her companion and whispered something. Both of them giggled, then again looked at him, then again giggled. What did they find comic about him? he wondered.

As he waited, in growing weariness and vexation, for the waitress to bring him the *spaghetti al sugo* and green salad of his order, Middleton surveyed the crowded scene. But he took care not to glance at the two women on his right, or at the solitary woman on his left.

All at once, an elderly, goblin-like Japanese, with thick, silvery hair brushed back over pointed ears, rose from his table and walked awkwardly, as though afflicted with arthritis of the hips, towards a table at which, stirring her coffee, a young woman slumped alone. Her triangular face had on it an expression of sullen weariness. But, as soon as it was clear that the Japanese was approaching her, it was as though a bright light had been shone on it.

The Japanese pointed to the vacant chair opposite to the girl and said something, inaudible to Middleton. '*Dozo, dozo!*' the girl replied, in what Middleton recognized as Japanese, not Korean, nodding vigorously and smiling. The Japanese lowered himself gingerly into the chair, as though any quick or abrupt movement would cause him pain; took up the menu; then put it down and leaned towards her, elbows on the table. He extended both his small hands. With a laugh she took them in her even smaller ones.

A short while later a couple, man and woman, arose from their table and decorously, she following behind him, wove their way between the tables to a door – not the one by which Middleton had entered – marked EXIT, below Korean characters which presumably said the same thing. Middleton turned to watch them as they passed through to the lift.

Soon after this couple had vanished from sight, two young men jumped up from their table and then, as though deliberately restraining their eagerness, sauntered, hands in pockets, to another table, in a distant corner, where a couple of young women in large straw hats were seated before long, empty glasses.

Suddenly it became clear to Middleton why the head waiter had brought him, past all those empty tables, to this crowded area out of sight behind the horseshoe-shaped bar. But he felt no gratitude to him. The years when, on a trip abroad, away from his wife, he eagerly sought out some adventure, were now far behind him.

He picked up his glass and drained the last of the wine in it. Then, as he tasted the sour liquid on his tongue – he would have done better to order sake or beer – he heard a high, metallic voice: 'Excuse me, sir. Excuse me!'

It was the woman in the thick glasses at the table to the left.

He turned his head, the glass still in his hand. 'Yes?' His tone and expression were both deliberately unfriendly.

She smiled, revealing good teeth. 'May I . . .?' With a hand raised palm upwards, she indicated the copy of the *Financial Times*, bought at huge expense from a stand in the hotel, which he had placed on the chair next to his own.

Reluctantly he nodded. Then he said grumpily: 'I can't imagine that it'll be of much interest to you.' It was not even of much interest to him. He had bought it only because it was the sole English newspaper on offer.

She half rose from her chair as he passed the paper over to her. 'Thank you, sir.' She gave a little bob, not dissimilar to the one given by the head waiter.

For a time she put on a show, lips pursed, of reading the front page. Then she looked up at him and laughed. 'You are right! Not very interesting. Or maybe it is interesting but my English is too poor.' She lowered the paper on to the table beside her. 'You are American?'

'No, I'm not American.' He hesitated. 'I'm English.'

'Ah, English!' She squealed with delight. 'English gentleman!'

Middleton went on with his eating.

'I love Englishmen. At university I had one English teacher. Professor Rhodes. Real English gentleman.'

'I'm not sure that I'm a real English gentleman.'

'You like Korea?'

'I don't know. I haven't been here long enough.'

'You have only just arrived?'

'Yesterday evening.'

Suddenly she was over at his table. 'May I please . . .?' But even as she said the words, she was lowering herself into the chair opposite him. 'It is easier to talk if I . . .'

Unsummoned, the waitress was coming over. She addressed the woman, who consulted the menu and then, tilting her head upwards, ordered one of the ice-creams so resplendently illustrated on its cover. As soon as this had arrived, she dug her spoon into it, a ferociously determined expression on her face, and then, sucking noisily on it, looked up with a smile. Well, she had an attractive smile, there was no doubt of that.

Between further spoonfuls gouged out of the towering edifice of multicoloured ice-cream cemented with frozen chocolate, she continued with her questions: about where he lived; about his wife and children and grandchildren; about what he was doing in Korea. When she learned that he was a doctor, she let out another squeal of delight. 'You are not businessman! That is good, *good*!'

'Oh, I'm not sure about that.'

So it went on. Middleton was offhand, unwelcoming, eventually even brusque. But nothing would deflect her, as she now put some intrusive question to him and now vouchsafed something about her own life. Eventually he wanted to shout at her: 'Oh, for God's sake shut up, *shut up*! I don't want to talk, not to you, not to anyone. I'm old. I'm jet-lagged. I'm tired after having given far too long a lecture. I want to finish this soggy spaghetti and this vinegary salad and whatever is left in the carafe of this disgustingly acid wine, and then I want to trudge up to bed and swallow a sleeping-pill and sleep and sleep and sleep. Alone.'

But he had never found it easy to be discourteous. For the past forty or so years his wife had been telling him that people imposed on him and used him, that he was far too gullible and accommodating, that for God's sake he must learn to be tough.

Eventually he called for the bill. Waiting for it, he stared in moody silence, his head turned away from her, at the horseshoe-shaped bar. Then all at once he felt her hand on the sleeve of his alpaca jacket. She tweaked it gently. 'Are you angry that I speak to you?'

'No, I'm not *angry*.' He all but added: 'Merely bored.'

'I must explain.' She placed her elbows on the table and then leaned across it. 'May I tell you story?' She did not wait for an answer. 'I am country girl. Father was farmer.'

Although her English was so poor, she told her story well. His bill now clutched in a hand, Middleton was first impatient, exasperated. Then, as though he were a child coaxed into swallowing some strange medicine against his will, he began to listen, became interested, eventually was moved.

She had been born when her numerous brothers and sisters – there were eight of them in all – were nearing adulthood and had most of them left the family farm in a remote cranny of the island of Cheju. Her parents had doted on her; but they had also been extremely strict, as they had never been with any other of their offspring. They had lavished money which they could ill afford on her education at private school. They had been determined that she should eventually go to university.

The farm sloped down to a river; and it was there that, one day, as she was watering the cows, she had seen a figure seated at an easel. He was wearing crimson trousers, high black boots, a black shirt and a black beret, tipped jauntily over an eyebrow. He had called out to the four-teen-year-old girl and reluctantly she had gone over to him, a bucket full of water in each hand. Slim, his narrow back erect as he sat on a canvas stool at his easel, he had, when seen from a distance, struck her as young; but now she saw that he was an old man, even older than her father, almost as old as her grandfather. He had held out a thermos flask. He was thirsty, this heat made one thirsty, he wanted to brew some ginseng tea. Could she possibly bring him some hot water?

Fortunately her mother and father were out. She filled the thermos with hot water and then, on an impulse, took one of the rice cakes which her mother had baked the day before and carried that too down to the old man by the river. He offered her some ginseng tea but she refused. She did, however, remain with him, squatting on the bank, while he drank his. In answer to her at first shy and then increasingly bold questioning, he told her that he was not a professional painter, only an amateur, even though he sometimes managed to sell his paintings. For many years an accountant in Seoul, he was retired now, living alone, a widower, in a one-room flat in Cheju City. His only son was in America, working in a Korean restaurant. The son was so busy that he seldom wrote and then only briefly.

She was touched and attracted by his loneliness. What had brought him to the river? she asked him. He shrugged. Chance, he said. He pointed to the ancient motor bike which he had propped against a tree. He explained how, without any plan, he mounted the motor bike and kicked it into life. Then he let it – he laughed, displaying uneven, brown teeth and purple gums – take him where it wished. Today it had taken him here. Again he laughed. For once the motor bike had shown good sense, he said. It had brought him to a kind and pretty girl.

From then on she would each day listen, wherever she was on the farm, for the roar and rattle of the motor bike. As soon as she heard it, she would find some excuse to go down to the river. The man was a wonderful talker, she said; he could have been a writer, he had many, many stories, some funny, some sad.

'Then we are lovers,' she said. 'Maybe you think that, because I am very young girl and he is old man, he . . . he – ' She sought for a word.

'Seduced me?' he supplied.

'Seduced me,' she repeated dubiously. 'But he is not bad man. He loves, I love.' She sighed. 'For me, first lover, first lover of my life. But he – he has many lovers before me.' Suddenly her round, pudgy face looked attractive, as she tilted her head sideways and away from Middleton, to stare across the room.

All at once he was reluctantly drawn to her, no longer feeling any exasperation or even weariness.

In a copse by the river they would make love – 'wonderful, wonderful love,' she sighed. 'I am happy, happy, happy. I do not care if mother and father find out. I care about nothing, nothing.'

One day she waited for the roar and rattle of the motor bike, waited all through a long summer's day, waited in vain. He never came. Nor did he come the next day. She thought, in despair, that perhaps he had tired of her. Then, after many anguished days of waiting, she saw, tucked away in the bottom corner of her father's newspaper, which she was using to light the kitchen fire, a brief paragraph about the old man's death. In Cheju City a motor bike had suddenly careered off the street into some pedestrians, killing a woman and seriously injuring a child. The passenger, an old man, had apparently suffered a heart attack. He too had been killed. The paper gave his name.

Her eyes had by now filled with tears. 'I could not stop thinking of him, day after day. Dead. I still think of him. I cannot love young man. I am not interested in young man. I want only man like him. Old man.' She placed her cheek, head turned sideways, on the arms which were resting on the table. She drew a deep sigh. 'Strange,' she said. 'Sad. Why do I love only old man? What am I to do?'

That was how Middleton eventually agreed to meet her the next day. He would be free in the afternoon, he told her; and she then said that she would show him over one of the palaces – 'Very historical, very beautiful.'

Before they said goodnight, he asked her for her name. 'Sukie,' she said. 'That is my name in English. In Korean it is Sook-hee.' She spelled it out for him very slowly, frowning as she did so, as though in an effort to remember the sequence of letters. 'S-O-O-K-H-E-E.'

After his lecture the next afternoon, the dean said to Middleton: 'Maybe we have some ginseng tea or a drink together? I am not busy – ' he looked dubiously at his watch – 'for forty, forty-five minutes.'

'Oh, that's very kind of you. But a friend has promised to take me sightseeing.' As he said the word 'friend', Middleton felt a sudden, unexpected explosion of joy within him.

'A friend? I thought you have no friends in Seoul.'

'Well, not really a friend. An introduction. Some friends in England gave me an introduction.'

'Korean introduction?'

Middleton hesitated. 'No. An, er, American businessman.'

Sukie was waiting for him in the lounge of the hotel. She was wearing a shiny purple dress, tight across the stomach and breasts and so short that it revealed her knobbly knees, dizzily high-heeled shoes, and a yellow straw hat, the brim of which flopped over her forehead as she jumped up from a bench to greet him with a shrill: 'Dr Middleton!' She looked unappealing, vaguely absurd. But yet again he felt that sudden, unexpected explosion of joy within him.

Joy soon turned to irritation. 'I will carry briefcase,' she said, putting out an arm.

'Why should you?'

'It is heavy for you.'

'Of course it isn't. Anyway, I can leave it at the desk. I don't need it. It has nothing in it but my lecture notes.'

When, in the garden of the palace, they came to a steep flight of steps, she solicitously took his arm in order to support him. He pulled away. But as her body touched his, he breathed in deeply the scent, muskily heavy, with which she must have drenched herself.

Constantly she asked him: 'Do I walk too fast?' Constantly she urged him: 'Let us sit here for a moment.'

Did she imagine that he was so old that he needed repeated assistance, repeated rests? For God's sake, did he look like an invalid? But as well as being exasperated by her concern for him, he was also moved – as he had been moved, in the Café Good Luck, by her grief for her dead lover.

That evening she took him to a small Korean restaurant, owned by cousins of hers. Still she fussed over him. Was he able to sit on the floor? Maybe it was too uncomfortable for him? Maybe he would like another cushion? Maybe he would like a back-rest? Would *kimchi* – the revolting pickled cabbage which Koreans seemed to devour at every meal – upset his digestion? Did he need a taxi to take him back to the hotel or could he manage the five minutes walk? Throughout that walk, she held on to his arm with both her hands, from time to time placing her cheek against his sleeve in what appeared to be both love and submission.

They were together again the next afternoon and evening, after he had first lectured at another university and then endured a tedious luncheon party given for him by its president.

This time it was in the Japanese restaurant of the hotel that they ate dinner. Sukie laughed at his clumsiness with chopsticks. 'No, no! I will show you, I will show you!' She took his chopsticks from him, picked up a piece of raw fish and then held it out to him. As she inserted it in his mouth and he then forced himself to swallow, he felt acutely embarrassed. He was sure that all the people around them, some of them Westerners, were watching them. 'Now you try! Try again!' She spoke to him like a schoolmistress to a pupil. Reluctantly he tried. The piece of fish fell off the chopsticks on to his shirt. She shrieked with laughter. 'Oh, Sam, Sam!' By now he had persuaded her to call him, not Dr Middleton, but by his Christian name.

When they left the restaurant, Sukie again took his arm; and again she pressed her face against the sleeve of his alpaca jacket. Then looking up at him, her eyes huge behind their glasses, she asked with simple candour: 'I come to bedroom now?'

Middleton hesitated. He shook his head. 'Better not, Sukie.'

She looked like a small child from whom an expected present has been suddenly and unaccountably withheld.

'Better not? Why better not?'

He did not answer.

Later, lying sleepless in his air-conditioned bedroom, he thought: You fool! You bloody fool!

The following day, they had luncheon together in the Café Good Luck. When, at one moment, laughing at something which he had told her about his favourite granddaughter, she leaned across the table to put her hand over his and then gently to squeeze it, he suddenly found that he was getting an erection. Now he wanted only to finish the meal and to take her upstairs.

'Will you come up to my bedroom now?' he leaned over to whisper to her, as she passed out ahead of him through the glass door which he was holding open for her.

Her smile was radiant: 'Of course! Yes! Yes!'

Clearly she knew the hotel well. It was better, she said, for them first to walk down to the basement, where the lavatories and telephones were situated. If they took the lift there, then no one at reception would see them. 'For me it does not matter,' she said. 'I do not care. But you are famous man, famous doctor. Maybe for you it is better not to be seen.'

In the lift she suddenly lowered a hand to his crotch, disconcerting him by her boldness. 'Why you refuse yesterday evening?' she asked in a teasing, coaxing voice.

'Because I was a fool.'

When she had undressed, he was amazed by the beauty of her breasts: large, rounded, firm. He had heard that silicone implants were far more common in the countries of the Far East, where breasts were naturally small, than in Europe. Could she have had such implants? He was no less amazed by the ferocious skill with which she made love to him. He rarely now made love to his wife and, when he did so, the love-making all too often ended not in ejaculation but in a weary: 'Let's just have a cuddle.'

Later, washing himself while, in the bedroom next door, she sang what he guessed to be a Korean folk-song in a high, clear voice, he remembered an incident from the previous year, when he had attended a medical conference in Bangkok. One of his colleagues, a young North Country gastroenterologist, had told the story, in the crowded bar of their hotel, of how he had picked up a Thai girl – 'She couldn't have been more than eleven or twelve. But, God, her technique was terrific! It was the fuck of a lifetime.'

At the time Middleton had been disgusted both by the story itself and by the crudity of the final phrase.

But now he thought: The fuck of a lifetime.

Yes, that was what it had been.

After they had dressed, Middleton said that he must buy his wife a present.

'You buy present because you feel bad?' she asked.

He was angry. 'Certainly not! I always take a present back for my wife after a trip abroad.'

'I come shopping with you?'

'Yes, of course! You can help me choose – and bargain for me. I can never bargain.'

Beneath the streets around the hotel, there stretched a subterranean labyrinth of stores. Her arm in his, Sukie led him from one to another. Clearly an experienced shopper, she repeatedly dissuaded him from this or that purchase. 'No good!' she would say. 'Look at stitching here!' Or: 'Too much, too much!' after she had failed to strike a bargain. Eventually, at amazingly low prices, he had bought a fake Longines watch for one of his two daughters, a silk nightdress for the other, and a fake Cartier handbag for his wife.

'This is beautiful bag,' Sukie said, as the shopkeeper rummaged for some wrapping paper. She picked it up and clicked it open. 'Beautiful. Like real Cartier.' She put it down and then picked up her own bag from the chair where she had placed it. She smiled down at it ruefully. 'This bag very old,' she said. 'Look.' She held it out to him.

Suddenly, on an impulse, he stretched across the counter and took another of the fake Cartier bags off it. 'For you,' he said. 'My present for you.'

She clapped her hands together. 'Oh, Sam, Sam!' she squealed. 'Truly for me? A bag like you give your wife?'

They returned to the hotel and once more made love. Then, while she was in the bathroom washing – once more he could hear her singing that Korean folk-song in her high, clear voice – Middleton got off the bed and tiptoed across to the chair on which the new bag was resting. Sukie had already transferred to it all the contents of her old one. He clicked the bag open, pulled two fifty dollars out of the back pocket of his trousers, and then inserted them in the purse inside the bag.

He would say nothing to her; he would let her find the money by herself.

*

The next morning the hotel restaurant was unusually crowded for breakfast, because of the arrival of a party of Germans. Middleton searched in vain for a table, walking up and down now one aisle and now another. Then he felt a tweak at the back hem of his jacket.

'Why not sit here?'

It was a sixtyish Englishman, with sparse greyish hair and a luxuriant greyish moustache cascading over his long upper lip, who had addressed him in the bar on the night of his arrival. Employed by a computer firm, he had already spent several weeks in the hotel.

'Oh! Oh, thank you.'

'What a row these Germans make! They never *say* things. They have to shout them.' The Englishman had a hoarse, nasal voice. On the table beside him was a rumpled paperback thriller. 'I'm a great reader,' he had confided to Middleton at their first meeting.

When Middleton had returned to the table from the buffet, the Englishman chewed on some toast and said, a malicious glint in his eyes: 'I saw you yesterday with our Sukie. In the Café Good Luck.'

Our Sukie? 'Yes, we were having lunch together.'

'No doubt, as usual, she chose all the most expensive things on the menu!' The Englishman's laugh snorted down his long nose. It sounded as though he were blowing it.

'Actually she ate very little.'

'That girl certainly gets around.' The Englishman leaned across the table. 'Did she feed you all that crap about the aged artist boyfriend, the one and only love, and about needing an old man to turn her on?'

Head lowered, Middleton began deliberately to scrape butter over a slice of toast.

'Well, I suppose if a tart is that unseductive, she has to have some gimmick for seduction. A successful one, a very successful one, one gathers. It flatters all us geriatrics. The other girls say she's never short of a client – or money. Men of our age are much more generous, I imagine, than young ones. We want to be, if only out of gratitude. And usually we can afford to be.' He sighed. 'Ah, well! She gave me a good time – until I got bored with her. She certainly knows her stuff. And – as you no doubt noticed – she has the most terrific tits!'

That afternoon Middleton almost did not keep his appointment with Sukie in the foyer.

When she thanked him effusively for the money placed in the handbag, he merely shrugged and snapped 'Oh, forget it!' When she now took his arm to assist him down the steps into the labyrinth of underground shops, he pulled free with an exasperated 'Oh, for God's sake!' When she once again asked, in one of the museums, 'You are tired? You wish to sit down?', he retorted angrily: 'No, I am not! And no, I do not!' At one moment she addressed him as 'Daddy' – 'Why is Daddy so cross with his little girl today?' Then he really exploded: 'What did you call me? Why the hell did you call me that? I am not, repeat not, your Daddy, and you are not, repeat not, my little girl. Thank God!'

She bit on her lower lip; her eyes blinked rapidly behind their thick glasses. 'Sorry.' She looked as if she were about to burst into tears.

'And whatever possessed you to choose those awful glasses?'

'Sorry?'

'If you have to wear glasses, why draw attention to it by choosing ones so large and ugly?'

'Sorry.' She repeated it: 'Sorry.'

They parted in the foyer of the hotel only a few minutes after nine. He was tired, he told her; he had to make an early start for the airport.

'Maybe I come up to bedroom just for short time?'

He shook his head.

'Just for few minutes. Yes?'

'No! I've told you, I'm tired, I have an early start. I must get a good night's sleep before that hellish journey.'

'As you wish.' She shrugged, clutching the fake Cartier bag tight against her stomach as though as a shield. Then she said: 'I will come to airport with you. What time you leave?'

'No, I'm afraid that won't be possible.'

'Not possible?'

'No. You see the dean of the medical faculty will be coming to see me off. He'll be coming in his car. It would be difficult to explain if you . . .' Suddenly he felt ashamed of his cruelty.

'So I say goodnight.' Her voice was weak, drained. She put her face up, as though for a kiss.

But he merely extended a hand, took her limp, reluctant one, and shook it.

'Goodbye, Sam!' she called after him.

He pretended not to hear her, as he continued to walk towards the lift.

When, shortly before seven o'clock, Middleton was about to clamber into the dean's car, he suddenly became aware that Sukie was standing, in her tight purple dress and dizzily high heels, the 'Cartier' bag under an arm, at the far end of the forecourt. He knew that she knew that he had seen her; but, getting into the car and slamming the door, he behaved as though he had not done so.

The dean was fiddling with the door of the boot. He seemed to be unable to lock it. Middleton drew a handkerchief out of a trouser pocket and mopped at his forehead. The sun was already high enough to make him sweat. Then, suddenly, he was aware that Sukie was racing towards him.

Her heels rattled like hail on the cement of the forecourt, louder and louder. Having reached the car, she stooped at the window, hands on knobbly knees, to stare in at him with an extraordinary mixture of grief, panic and anger.

Briefly Middleton stared back, then looked away.

But almost at once he was overmastered by a mysterious compulsion to look again at her. He could not help it, he had to do so. As their gazes locked, she put up a hand and tore off those hideous glasses. Her eyes, huge and dark, were gazing into his. Her mouth stretched and crumpled. Then tears welled out from the eyes and rolled down her cheeks.

That could not be acting, could not!

The dean clambered into the seat beside Middleton. He peered across, bewildered, at the stooping woman. He seemed about to say something, then clamped his mouth shut.

The car began to move.

'I hope you have enjoyed your visit,' the dean said.

'Yes. Yes. Oh, yes. Thank you.'

Middleton twisted his body round, to look over his shoulder, out of the rear window.

'Is everything all right?' the dean asked.

Sukie had vanished.

'Yes, thank you. Yes. Everything is fine.'

Jack Says

DEBORAH LEVY

I'll have a beer an my tart wants a coke. I'll tell ya somethin to cheer you up – anyone want a deep pan seafood pizza? No? Thass a shame cuz I just seen some bloke puke one up near here.

What pleasant weather we're havin folks! My name's Jack an that was number one an two of my ten forms.

Dontcha all wanna go on holiday with me? But I tell you what. I own a big library, a couple of oscars an a bottle of Bison vodka in the freezer – whoops I just shat myself. Anyone got a piece of kitchen roll? No? Whass the world comin to? Where's my PA? The one wit chemicals in her hair an flirty hips – has she got somethin for me to wipe myself? I like the dark at the movies. I specially like the usherette at my local cinema. She's got sad eyes an a built up shoe where her leg's too short, an she comes over all shy when she tells me how much she likes my films.

Hey, sad-eyed movie buff, I knows you like my movies, but do you like me? Whass your name?
– Ssssssssssarah. Poor gal stutters like she's gonna barf on her shoe.
– Whal Sarah, I says, you is a sweet girl an I wish you the best in life.

– Fuck you. She got no stutter this time.

– I'm as sweet as your rancid arse pal an you aint the record sleeve cover you thinks you is.

P'haps she don't like me after all? Never wanted a foul-mouthed woman to be the mother of my children anyway.

What do I want? I want Susan. Jack an Susan forever. Carved in the apple tree. J an S traced with a finger on a pile of cocaine, on margarine, on my car windscreen as I put my foot down an slide past the slow cocksuckers who don't understand a car is not an armchair. This is how Suze got inside me.

I'm sittin with my babe Linda in a bar, Night Jet it was called an we is drinkin cocktails. She sees my attention a wanderin thataway to a beehive brunette all lazy blue eyes an a gash of white panties 'tween her womanly thighs an this gorgeous criture, she's recognized me. Not from magazines an TV interviews, she's met me in her head. Like she knows me. She knows I want to play with her architecture. So her lip's curlin she's nervous, excited, an she's givin me that look an I thinks – you're all right there – I'm stoned, bin smokin an I catch Linda sippin her cocktail an she sort of looks like my mother. She's sittin opposite me with her hand on my cock an her tits pushin towards me an I want her to die. I'm thinkin I gotta chuck her an while I'm plottin how to murder sexy mother girl-friend Linda an how to fuck hotstuff beehive brunette, Linda pulls me back to herself, back to her girlfriend self an she smashes her cocktail glass an she carves an X into her flesh through her stockins. In front of my eyes she does this – blood runnin down her nylons an I says BABY cut that out. She says, I just did Jack. I says Go an destroy yerself somewhere else cunt.

Now the beehive brunette she sees this from her bar stool an she's eatin peanuts real cool. She waves at me an I go over to her, it's like she's got a menthol aura an she's lickin peanut salt off her fingers.

– Hi Boy Terror, she says. That poor messed up chick of yours should find some other expression.

She swings her leg nearer to my crotch an I'm not quite ready for her.

She wants me. But I dunno what is the me she wants. To give myself time I buy her a drink an she aint smilin no more.

– I bet you look jus like your old man when you is a pensioner, she says.

– Why do you say that hotstuff?

– All youz beatniks look jus like your daddies.

– Whass your name?

– Susan.

– So Susan. My name's Jack. How come you thinks you knows me so well an we jus swapped sex looks thass all?

– Whal, like I knows you intimately, says she.

– What's this knowledge you has then Suzie scholar?

She's drawn to me, kinda curious an repelled.

Ice blue eyes. She's travellin my body with those eyes an I'm shiverin. She jus keeps on goin. They're fixed now on my shirt, I never wear yellow – p'haps I look stupid, don't wear colours usually. Her eyes, like the steel of a doctor's stethoscope on my skin, they make me hold my breath cuz she holds them steely cold gainst my body, there an there, she's travellin my legs an shoes an back to my eyes an I say into her menthol blue cool a bit dazed cuz I vision her plantin things on the moon, long an lithe bendin over puttin seeds into craters, an she's got no knickers on an she has a glass of malt whisky in her hand, rain fallin into her glass an she says – I like my whisky with water. It is wondrous this reverie but I'm scarin myself so to lighten up I come back to the Night Jet bar an I growl like a pimply bike boy.

– Do you think my sideburns are too long?

I don't wait for her to answer cuz I'm visionin her again. She got steel blades on the soles of her shoes an she's walkin on a pond iced over holdin a white cat in her arms, there are four eyes lookin at me – cat's eyes an hers cuz her gaze is four eyes deep – an she's also just sittin there checkin me out.

She hates me. She wants me.

– When you look at me what do you see hotstuff Suzie?
– Girls pukin in their panties Jack my sweet.

She's gonna kill me. She wants to punish me. I want her to.

– Quit that hang dawg expression Jack the laddo. I'll fuck with you whatever. RELAX.

She's gonna do me damage but I'm undone, she's sussed the fear in me an she's ridin it.

– Honey, I say like I've known her for years, come with me to a party. I don't want to go alone. I'm feelin sick. Do I look OK?
– Yeah. You look OK an your sideburns are jus right.
– Come with me babe.
– What kind of party?
– Just sittin round a table eatin stuff. I hate makin conversation. Please come.
– OK.

Oh boy! I buy us another round an I take her fingers put em in my mouth cuz they're salty. From the peanuts. I suck em slow an she reads the beer mat all the time shovin more of her fingers into my mouth an she's feelin my gums an teeth an I can see her in profile, her blue eye-lashes makin flutter shadows over the beer mat, the light catchin her beehive, turnin her hair pink, all tits an legs, her fingers in my mouth an I'm gonna be the life an soul of the party tonight.

Mel-an-chol-ia! I stuff potato an white fish an carrots an broccoli an breadroll into my mouth, chew, open my mouth, wide, wider, wider – look! look! look! Finger pointin at my saggin mouth. Look! Everyone looks at the mush dribblin down my chin. Melan-cholia. Melan-choli-aaaaaaah – thass me screaming. Jack is screamin with his mouth open. Where's my fork or has somebody got it up their arse? Anyone want a big French sausage I got one here in my pants jus bustin for a chewin. Hey darlin take out ya teeth put them in that glass of Muscadet an I'll serve it to ya with mustard. Melan-cholia melan-cholia melan-cholia – sorry fatty I says to the woman on my right about to leave the table, but we're all middle class here aint we sweetheart? Thass right, what a luvely lump of stilton our host has provided for us, I agree wit you so what ya lookin so glum for eh? We all know about paro-dy here don't we? We all know men are sickos. I'm a givin you access to my unreconstructed male geology. Whooooh big words, take out yer penis, I mean pens ho ho ho aren't I the comedian – yep this is number three of my ten forms. What a roarin silence as they say in Highgate, kiss me quick, no not there, only dogs an aris-tocrats do that – cat gotcha tongue? OK – less get sensitive – anyone here got somethin to say about the poet Dryden? No? Howz about, you'll like this one, howz about, dum dum dum da Conrad? Aw come on cocksuckers fill it quick, this total lack of words – hooo look at her – she's gone purple this woman in Monsoon silk – your name's Joanna ain't it? Melan-cholia melan-choliaaaaah! No fraulein, don't go, be brave like my gorgeous girl here wit the buzzin beehive, she's gonna sleep with me whatever I do! Joanna you're mutterin somethin into your moustache, spit it out say your feelins, speak your mind like my Suzie here, don't go Joanna wallop me with your napkin – hoooo did she say somethin 'bout being rude? Who? Baby tell me an I'll nail their bollocks to the stripped floorboard. Joanna baby tell us whass wrong. Somethin upset you? Is there a shrink in the house? Someone to undo offence? Tell us about yer childhood injuries. Perhaps it's the world situation thass brought on the tears? I know. I know. It's frightenin aint it Joanna. Never know who you'll meet at a dinner party – a no go zone some of em – aint that right babe, best to be alert, look to the left anythin happenin there? Is that young man in his tight arsed tweed jacket an axe murderer? An now to the right, see who's drinkin the Chateau Lafitte an nibblin the ciabatta with dangerous nuance. Hey Jason? I think you're gonna hit me! Well done you poof. Woooooo – here we go. Thank you Jason. Again. Again. There's a kind boy. Put me out of my misery. Please.

Put me out of my misery. I'm lyin in bed with Suzie an she's reading a newspaper with tortoiseshell spectacles perched on her nose which is crooked. It's sexy that broken nose an I'm holdin her hand an we made the best love ever, man it was aeroplanes hoverin over the runway, hares runnin fast into the floodlights; thass what it was like, she made me scream an she said you're so beautiful Jack – so that I never got room to tell her she was beautiful an she seemed to like that. She wanted to read, to make phonecalls, to take a shower an come back to bed. She wanted to brush out her hair an she wanted to sleep some more. Not lyin on me or anythin. Curved away from me an when I leaned over to kiss her she told me to get off her an then she woke up an we kissed. Oh man, we kissed. So now I'm just lyin there lookin at the ceilin. Make me breakfast Boy Terror, she says. I'll have poached egg on toast an a cuppa.

Suzie. I'm gonna do number six of my ten forms while you eat your egg with those narcotic lips of yours, black pepper for you my sweet an lashins of butter on your toast. Tea OK? A little more milk? You've reduced me to teacuppery. We talk teapots an sugar an Marmite an jam. But I'm revvin up now. I'm almost there. Ready steady go! I'm six years old an I'm ridin my bicycle on the pavement. There's a cat lyin on her side in the sun an she's chasin flies, little jabs with her paw an she's got teats with cat milk in em. I just keep on cyclin an I ride over her. I ride over her belly. I squash her, all of her, she's heavy an yelpin an I can't stop.

Suzie's bent over the tuna, tin opener in her hand, still hungry. Insatiable Suzie.

My precious, I love fuckin you. I like the way you open that tin of tuna. She's got dark rings under her eyes, still in her shorts an it's winter.
– My fucked up fuck, she says, spoonin the tuna into her mouth.

Suze is my dream girl. She's blown me away. I want to put my hands on her but I've gone shy. I want Suze to put me out of my misery. I want her. I want her. I want her. Push against me baby. Open your legs, oh oh oh . . . I've spilled my cyberseed on to her stomach an she says – that's nice.

I was nearly gonna go into number nine of my ten forms but I feel a love attack comin on.
– Suze, I want to ask you somethin dangerous. Don't be offended. If you think I've gone too far just say so OK?

– OK.
– Less go down Tescos do a weekend shop?
Suze shakes her head.
– No way Jacko. I don't do that kinda stuff wit you. Tell
me your number nine instead.

She is my precious chosen woman. We have known each
other's bodies for three months now. Sometimes I ring her
apartment an she's not there. I'm panickin. She's away for
weeks at a time an I'm lonesome without her. But she
always sends me postcards an signs herself S with two
lines through it, like a dollar. She's warm an distant, she
says she hates perfume, that perfume is old-fashioned.
She is the woman I murmur into pillows with. Yes, she is.
I'm panickin. How'm I gonna keep my Suze in my arms?
I tell her number nine.

Back in the Night Jet bar. I'm a psychopath in a smart suit,
heart beatin gainst my shirt cuz Suzie might just walk
away an never come back. I test her affection for me. I tell
her weird things that come into my head an I don't tidy
em up – make em cute or clever or pretend they're civilized, an she don't stomp off, she strokes me an drinks
Diet Pepsi. We come out the other side an I'm nearer
heaven than I ever dreamed. Then she takes a break.

Yep I'm panickin alright. I'm gonna do number seven of
my ten forms in the Night Jet bar. I gotta sore throat an
nobody cares.

Suze has always got somethin to read in her bag. Anywhere we go, she just reads. Fashion magazines. Journals.
A paperback. She sips her beer an reads an then she comes
back to me. Sometimes she just watches me or asks me to
tell her a joke. What if she don't like me no more?

– Hey, I says, an she turns her thrillin eyes on me, the
eerie blue of lagoons that have had chemicals dropped in
em.
– Go on Jacko, strut your stuff.
– Whal Suzie, I'm thinkin bout this broad I used to go with
an she drew portraits in charcoal, kind of depressed she
waz but a beauty. One day I come home late from filmin
cuz I waz fuckin someone more cheerful an less bootiful
than she, an she has a stick of black charcoal in her fingers.
It drops on the floor an it breaks into dust an she says that
she knows the charcoal dust on the floor is the black flecks
of hurt in her green eye.

In the Night Jet bar there's this contraption by the cocktail mixers for catchin flies. It flickers on an off an if there
aint no music playin an there is no one speakin it sounds
like the end of the world. Now I jus hear the fly catcher
crackle, an when I catch Suzie's profile I sees she got some
kind of rash on her cheek.

– Yesterday, I wakes up my Suze an I thinks Jack you're
this country's most dedicated freedom fighter. You should
be given the revolutionary salute. Nearly comin up to bus
pass age an you is still a free man wit a free dick in a free
economy wit a cheese flan for one in the freezer. Suzie asks
the barman for some prawn flavoured crisps. Today she's
wearin jeans an red boots. She's three pence short an I'm
just goin through the change in my pocket when the barman says, forget it. He's gay an handsome. Probably forty
but he looks like he's twenty-five, mixin cocktails like
thass what he was born to do. Suze eats her crisps watchin
him shake up a margarita.

Shake shake shake. Barman rattlin the ice, rimmin the
glass with salt.

How come Boy Terror, she says, you talk like a beatnik
cowboy? I mean you are bourgeois French an educated at
the Sorbonne?

– Whal Suze, says I, thass cuz this bastard Americun style be number eight of my famous ten forms.

The barman smiles.

– Cut his dick off Suze.

– Pass me that little knife you cut the lemons with then, she says.

She's undoin the buttons on my fly. Tinker tailor soldier, sadist, faggot, martian, rebel-dyke.

– Hey I like your boxer shorts Jacko.

Her cold hands wriggle the cotton off my hips.

Barman wipes the lemon juice off the knife with a dish-cloth an gives it to her, all the time sayin somethin like triple sec is better than cointreau for a margarita but we've run out.

I like this feelin. Her hands on me.

– Whass that rash on your cheek Suze?

– Oh that. Yeah. It's measles.

– Measles? Only kids get measles.

– Yep, she says, takin out my dick, playin with it, runnin the silver blade turned flat on its side down my love pump, still eatin her crisps.

– I caught measles from the child inside you Jack. Now then Bob, she says to the barman, shall I cut his dick off, or shall I cut his hand off?

– My hand, I says. She giggles.

– Why's that Boy Terror?

– There's more psychic tension in my dick.

Bob hands her the margarita but she's laughin too much to take it, laughin an smotherin my cheek wit kisses. She puts the knife down an I put my dick back inside my pants an we talk through some ideas I got for my next movie. After a while she picks up her bag an goes off to meet her best friend Sarah, the usherette with the built-up shoe, for a curry.

All lonesome again. Thass right folks! Gotta cheese flan

for one in the fridge. Gonna eat it on the sofa with my underpants on my head. Sets me a thinkin 'bout the one an only time I did a spell of film actin. Me an this man star, whass his name? Forgotten. Anyhow I'd bin smokin some motherfuckin stuff an the director says OK guys, we gonna improvise this scene, ready? So we do our bit an this director walks over, taps me on the shoulder an says can we have a word Jack? Sure says I. What you did was good he says, thing is the movie's set in seventeen eighty nine an they didn't say 'man' all the time them days.

Bob's got this mean sly smile on his perfect face.
– So Jack. Heard you say you got ten forms. How many you done so far?
– 'Bout seven, says I.
– Whass happened to the other three?
He's servin someone else while he talks. Some guy wit a checked shirt starin at the fly catcher. When he gives him his drink their hands touch. Kinda intimate. A lotta stuff in that touch. Man, I want some of that stuff. The kinda small touchin you do with your chosen one. I give Bob a big tip when I pay for my drink. Too big. He turns his back on me as I make my way home to watch the cartoons on TV. That small touchin's upset me. Think I can feel number ten comin on! Somethin involvin torture an deep kissin.

Heron Cottage

SHENA MACKAY

The sisters really had no business to be in Heron Cottage that afternoon. They spoke in whispers at first, half-expecting to hear the sharp crack of a stair and Miss Martin's voice demanding what on earth they thought they were doing in her kitchen, although they knew that she was lying in the secret, unthinkable chamber at the back of T.H. Lovelock and Sons, Undertakers and Funeral Directors. Yet they felt a camaraderie, as if they were engaged on some prank that the fifteen years between their ages had denied them until now. Miss Martin's string shopping bag, with a wisp of dried onion skin caught in its mesh, hung from a hook on the door, and a red vinyl cook's apron garnished with tomatoes. A present, Rosamund supposed, she had never seen Miss Martin cooking anything. But not so incongruous after all perhaps, for the apron advertised Heinz tomato soup, and presumably Miss Martin dined on the few vegetables she grew.

Rosamund, the elder of the trespassers, Esmée Martin's nearest neighbour, had been entrusted years ago with a key for use in an emergency. This was the second time she had used it. The first had been the horrible afternoon when, realizing she had not seen Miss Martin about for some time, she had found her in bed, delirious and dehydrated, and had had to call an ambulance.

The funeral was to be held the day after the sisters let themselves in, and such family as Miss Martin had were arriving in the evening to spend the night at Heron Cottage. Rosamund had suggested, and would have been dissuaded easily had Lucy not agreed with such alacrity, that they should pop round and tidy up a bit for the bereaved, if distantly related, family. Rosamund wondered how much her impulse owed to guilt and neighbourliness, and how much to a wish to entertain Lucy who was on a visit from London.

'There may be things going bad in the fridge,' she had said. 'And the beds should be aired.'

Her voice had sounded too hearty to her, brazen and tactless, as if she had spoken of decomposition and the sheets of a deathbed and the waiting bed of cold clay in the spring rain, but Lucy had been excited at the prospect of entering Miss Martin's house. She had only glimpsed her in the garden, and reading the obituaries had been surprised to learn that the old thing had been quite a well-known poet in her day, and regretted now not having pursued the acquaintance. Ros might have asked her to tea or drinks, she thought, sure that Miss Martin would have warmed to her. The faded deckchair, the ancient panama at dusk, night-scented stocks, assumed in memory the poignancy of a thousand lost summer evenings.

Rosamund and Lucy had driven into Sevenoaks early to buy food suitable for Miss Martin's Londoners at the deli. It had been Lucy's idea to leave them the makings of an evening meal and breakfast.

'Shouldn't we get some baked meat?' she had asked, noticing a glistening purple knob of bone protruding from a yellow-crumbed ham. 'Isn't that what you're supposed to have at funerals?'

Rosamund, catching sight of herself, so much older and stockier and wiser and wearier than her sister, in the glass above the counter, rolled her eyes heavenwards and told Lucy: 'They're not having anybody back to the cottage afterwards. Just everybody going to the pub.'

It seemed bleak and unsatisfactory, and she feared it would all peter out in embarrassment.

Now, in Miss Martin's kitchen with its scrubbed wooden draining-board and stone sink, the aconites outside shivering in the sun, she set the trendy old-fashioned brown paper carrier bag from the deli on the table and opened the little fridge. Apart from a carton of milk, which vindicated her, and an unopened packet of butter, it was quite empty.

'It's colder inside than out,' said Lucy. 'Aren't those celandines pretty? *She* would have loved them . . .'

'They're aconites. She did.'

Pneumonia aggravated by malnutrition. It was all so hideous. And unnecessary. How could she not feel silently accused? But it really hadn't been her fault. Everybody knew Esmée Martin was practically a recluse and fiercely independent. And she'd been as fit as a fiddle the last time Rosamund had seen her. Nobody could have seen how thin she was under that great duffle-coat, and she wasn't even particularly old. You didn't expect someone of sixty-odd to pop off like some hypothermic pensioner.

Rosamund, in an old navy blue jersey discarded by one of her sons, quilted waistcoat and jeans, sat down on a wooden chair at the scrubbed table and swept the fallen pollen from the dead catkins in the yellow jug into a neat heap. Rosamund had never been in Miss Martin's house without admiring some seasonal twigs, leaves, flowers or berries: old roses in an old Sheffield bowl, red poppies in a green jug, ox-eye daisies in white, cornflowers in blue glass, a crazed pink vase of spindleberries.

Lucy, who was closing a drawer of calm bleached tea towels, had affected, for her stay in the country, a style not unlike Miss Martin's own; she wore an oatmeal sweater over two print frocks, one half-unbuttoned, and a pair of flat-heeled boots. Now she was pulling open the doors of a wooden cupboard. She jumped back as something crashed down and rolled across the floor.

'Lucy!'

'Well, well, well! Take a look at this!'

Lucy retrieved, and held up a jar of peaches in brandy while the sun streamed through its glass and spilled golden juice on to the floor.

The shelves of the cupboard were stocked, stacked, brimming, with exotica; rose pouchong and Earl Grey and Lapsang Souchong tea, chocolate Bath Olivers, *langues de chat*, angels' trumpets, brandy snaps, marzipan and glacé fruits, coffee beans and chocolate coffee beans, little plum puddings, Turkish cigarettes. Bottles glittered in the darkness of the shallow cellar.

'Well! The stingy old . . .' Rosamund struggled to articulate the scraggy, scrawny, *old-fashioned* thing that was in her mind, '. . . boiling fowl! When I think of all those Tetley teabags! One was lucky to be offered a Happy Shopper bourbon! You would imagine, looking at this lot, that every day had been Christmas in Heron Cottage.'

'You don't suppose,' said Lucy, 'that it was for someone special? No, perhaps not . . .'

As the sisters dismissed the possibility of any romantic explanation for the hoard, Lucy had a regretful glimpse of herself seated at the kitchen table, nibbling an exotic biscuit and nodding sagely at some confidence. She followed Rosamund into the front room and found her kneeling in front of the big ugly old radiogram, opening the doors of its cabinet. Rosamund lifted out friable black records in brittle brown sleeves and laid them on the carpet.

'I'd never have taken her for a jazz fan,' she said. 'These must be worth a bob or two.'

'Curiouser and curiouser,' Lucy said. 'Do we really ever know anybody else? If they were digitally remastered . . .'

Rosamund pictured Esmée sitting on her stoop with a blue black voice and a trumpet wailing 'I hate to see that evenin' sun go down' over the darkening garden, and sitting on, damp with dew until her white head was a reflection of the white moon. And yet she had never heard that music pouring from the cottage or seen Esmée sitting so.

At a pang of, could it be, jealousy, she said, suddenly peevish, 'Well, we might have saved ourselves the trouble. There's enough food here to feed six times the number of people who'll be coming tomorrow. Even if they couldn't be bothered with the old girl when she was alive.'

She returned to the kitchen and picked up their carrier bag, and added defiantly one or two items from Esmée's store.

'Just like Miss Haversham . . .' Lucy was murmuring to the stopped clock.

'Havisham. I'm surprised at you, Lucy!'

She locked the door behind them and they stepped out into Miss Martin's garden where Miss Martin's spring cabbages grew. Lucy pulled open the door of the little shed, and a small wicker hamper tumbled out at her feet. The shed was stacked with empty Christmas hampers. They stared. Then Rosamund, outfaced by the baskets, touched the fallen one with her toe.

'This might come in handy. Bring it, Lucy, it won't be missed. What do you want to do about lunch?'

'"Gimme a pigfoot and a bottle of beer",' Lucy quoted from one of Miss Martin's records.

'Pub all right then?'

Although they'd be there again tomorrow. The funeral baked meats they had bought in the deli would come in handy for supper.

Suddenly Rosamund stopped on the path that led through the field to her own house.

'What's that you've got there? What are you hiding under your jersey? Show me at once!'

Lucy, blushing as deep a pink as the blighted, half-opened rose that had hung on the hedge all winter, drew out a bundle of letters and postcards, secured by a thick rubber band.

'How *could* you? How could you be so – shabby? If that's what living in London's made of you . . .'

A dozen secret urban shames stained Lucy darker red.

'It's people like you, your rotten Thames Water Board taking our water that nearly killed our river for ever!' Rosamund was going on, slightly incoherent with anger, as Lucy shouted, 'I'm going to put them back! I just thought they might give a clue! You can take them back yourself when you go to air the beds, which you seem to have forgotten was the main purpose of our visit!'

A gurgling to their left proved that the spring rains had saved the river but Rosamund was too enraged to hear it. Lucy broke away and ran to the house, and up the stairs to her bedroom, and stood panting against the white-painted latched door. She heard Rosamund come into the kitchen, and start banging about in the larder. Lucy lay face downwards on the faded patchwork quilt on her bed and eased the rubber band from the letters. She pulled out a postcard of Masaccio's *La cacciata dal Paradiso Terrestre*, Adam and Eve in agony, and turned it over, looking first at the signature. Edward.

What do the dead feel when they watch the living paw-ing through their precious possessions, the fleshy curious fingers' invisible acid etching the papers that testify to the dead one's tenancy in this world? Should Esmée Martin have been observing this young woman sprawled

on her sister's spare bed, an impulse towards an impossible, incorporeal lunge and snatch might have stirred the
air; or perhaps Esmée watched Lucy as dispassionately
as did the cross-stitched sampler on the wall above her.
After all, Esmée might have thought, with now-lofty
detachment, that thin bundle of cards and letters seemed
too slight to bear the suspended weight of half a lifetime's longing.

'This can't be it. This can't be all there is.' Lucy stared at
a card with 1967 postmarked across a Helvetian stamp.
'I wish you could see it – beautiful wild flowers and
wonderful cakes . . .'

'Wonderful cakes?' Was this a message from a man sick
with love among the gentians and edelweiss of the Alps?
Patently not: why then had Esmée preserved it; with not
so much as a bleached petal to speak of passion? Lucy
hated him, this heartless eater of cakes. He had not loved
Esmée Martin at all.

Esmée had read it as 'cakes' too, once, and wept. Much
later, she had seen that the word, in his careless scrawl,
was 'lakes', but by then she had realized that his feelings
for her were nothing like hers for him, and her mind's eye
retained a picture of Edward sitting on a chalet balcony
jutting into a postcard-blue sky, with a froth of *café au lait*
on his moustache and a big Swiss gateau in his hand. He
wore *lederhosen* whose braces were appliquéd with hearts
and flowers, and his bare knees touched the walking-skirt
of a laughing woman seated at his table; sunshine, glittering off white peaks, gilded two alpenstocks lolling
together against the carved wooden railing, making twin
dazzling suns of their encircled spikes. 'Cuckoo Cuckoo
Cuckoo' mocked the little bird in the clock on Esmée's
kitchen wall, although technically she could not be cuck-
olded, and the man was married to someone else.

*

Lucy extracted the very first letter, sent from Cadogan Square:

> 'My dear Miss Martin
> I know I have no right to write to you in this way, but since we met last night at the Ansteys', I have not been able to put you out of my mind. I shall be at the National Gallery tomorrow at three, in front of Watteau's "La Gamme d'Amour". I shall wait for one hour. If you do not wish to meet me, I would ask your forgiveness of my presumption in hoping that you felt as I did.
>
> Edward Leyland.'

'My dear love,' the second letter read, 'You have made me happier than any man deserves or dreams to be . . .'

There was an antique valentine embossed with twin doves in beribboned paper lace, which Lucy pressed to her own lips with a sigh, and thereafter a bunch of cards with brief messages – 'Usual place at seven' – 'Tomorrow' – 'Tuesday' . . . and then a sad handful of apologies for meetings missed, cancelled outings, plans gone awry. Lucy sensed the death of love as she read them.

Folded and refolded very small, creased as if it had been crumpled in despair and then straightened again, and its ink blotched and blurred, a last letter fell on to the bed. Lucy deciphered its closing words through a mist of her own tears – '. . . until then. One day, when you have forgotten all about me, you will see a tall man walking up your cottage path with his arms full of flowers, and you will wonder who this stranger can be, but just for a moment, until he sees your face at the window and breaks into a run, and drops his silly flowers as he opens his arms to hold you in them once more . . .'

Lucy cried, because he had never come up the path of Heron Cottage with his flowers, and for herself because there had been nothing in her own life to match Esmée Martin's love or tragedy, and she felt an emptiness and tawdriness and dissatisfaction with all her unromantic lovers. She wanted Esmée Martin's past, the lonely longing, the dashed hopes of the woman who had half-starved herself, and saved up for Christmas hampers so that she might produce a feast at a moment's notice, sustaining her thin body on rich products past their sell-by dates, who had risen early each morning to keep her house spotless and tend her garden in case he should appear, who had played her sad records as the moon rose, and faced her chaste bed at the death of another day with a prayer that the dawn would bring a stranger who was not a stranger.

Lucy put on her coat and slipped the correspondence into her pocket. Rosamund was in the kitchen, loading some dull husbandly garments into the washing machine. Lucy suddenly felt sorry for her.

'We'd better get going, if we're having lunch at the pub,' said Rosamund.

'I'm just going to put those things back,' said Lucy. 'I didn't read them, by the way.'

Rosamund smiled. 'I'm glad,' she said.

Lucy glanced up, through Esmée Martin's window, and saw a tall man walking up the path, a sheaf of lilies in his arms white and gold against his black coat. She opened the front door and the stranger took off his hat, revealing thick silver hair.

'Good afternoon,' he said. 'I was so sorry to hear the news. Are you one of the family?'

Lucy shook her head.

'I wonder if I might come in?' he asked.

Lucy saw that he was a straight-backed, vigorous-looking man. She stepped back, holding the door for him.

'I'm – I was – a very close friend of Esmée,' she told him.

'So was I. There are some things of mine, some letters, I believe, that she would have wished me to have. Of sentimental value only – of no interest to anyone else.'

An authorized biography of Esmée Martin materialized in the air between them, and vanished.

'I understand,' she said. 'Those lovely lilies should be put in water at once. For tomorrow. Shall we have a drink while I find your – letters? Esmée prided herself on keeping a nice little cellar . . .'

'Really?' He looked surprised. 'I'm Edward Leyland, by the way. I'm afraid I shan't be able to stay for the funeral.'

'Lucy Pierce.'

She held out her hand, which he pressed, while smiling into her eyes.

Lucy smiled back, letting her hand linger in his.

'I'm staying with my sister,' she said. 'Rosamund . . .' who would have to wait, because Lucy had not decided yet whether she should have some of the romance that had been Esmée's, or if Edward Leyland was to be made to atone for the waste of a life.

The Good Butler

TONY PEAKE

Ralph Goodall started swimming the morning after his fortieth birthday. He'd always planned to avoid the clichés of ageing, but as the years proliferated, so the attraction he felt for younger men intensified, and in helpless thrall to this burgeoning obsession, so he began, unfavourably, to compare the sleekness of their hard, enticing bodies with the progressive softening of his own. Not that anyone else – least of all his regular drinking companions, John and Henry – shared his disquiet. Still enviably lean, and always dapper, Ralph looked to them as slick and trim as he'd always looked. Yes, his barbered beard was now flecked with grey, and yes, the primness of his mouth was bracketed by lines, but the clean, sharp cut of his face and figure belied any need to worry.

'Hyper-sensitive, dear,' John would murmur, casting a rueful, downward glance at the Falstaffian swell of his own ungovernable body. 'Neurosis. That's what you have to guard against. Not blubber.'

And Henry, who had, in addition to all the major musicals, the entire Gilbert and Sullivan canon by heart, would hum in camp reassurance: 'She may very well pass for twenty-nine in the dusk with a light behind her.'

But Ralph knew otherwise. Lying full length in the bath, he would roll what excess fat he had between finger and thumb and note with dismay the way it puckered;

and when he stepped out of the tub, he had only to turn to the mirror for further, more spiteful proof of the advancing years: the striated sagging of a once pert bottom.

'Maybe it is neurotic,' he pouted at his reflection, 'but those who only serve have a duty to do so decorously.'

So, at ten thirty on the morning after his birthday, armed with a photograph and proof of his address, he presented himself at the Victorian baths round the corner from his flat.

Although he'd lived in the area fifteen years, and passed the baths every day on his way to and from the houses where, in the course of duty, he waited table, he'd never ventured inside. Wisely, too, was his first reaction. After the Victorian swank of their Gothic exterior, the foyer was a distinct disappointment. Modernized some time in the sixties (and probably not renovated since, thought Ralph) it seemed intent on distancing itself from the building it inhabited, on disclaiming its provenance, and thus providing an appropriately seedy setting for the tatty vending machine, the rows of fly-blown notices, and last but not least, the woman behind the ticket desk, who, if her thinning beehive was anything to go by, dated from when the foyer had last enjoyed the attentions of a decorator. Such was the air of desolation about this woman that Ralph felt impelled to chatter brightly about the weather as she filled in his details on the form. Not that he need have bothered. She didn't appear to hear a word he said, and as soon as she'd issued his card, returned her tired attention to the dogeared paperback at her elbow.

'And the changing room?' queried Ralph.

Without lifting her eyes from her book, but in tones made mercifully precise by her obvious reluctance at having to impart this information yet again, the woman said: 'Down the corridor and on your left.'

The corridor was narrow and badly lit. Halfway along its dim, oppressive length, Ralph came to a swing door made of heavy plastic, and pushing it open, found himself in a high-ceilinged room that, for all its unexpected loftiness, was every bit as cheerless as the rest of the building. The tiled floor was grimy and cracked, there was a scattering of sodden towels on the line of slatted seats that bisected the room, and half the metal lockers that stood against the walls were keyless.

Ralph grimaced, and skirting the puddles on the floor, stepped past the only other occupant of the room – a man in his eighties struggling into a pair of underpants designed for someone twice his size – and made for the bank of lockers against the far wall, where he quickly undressed and, with a pleased sense of aptness, put his neatly folded clothes into locker 40, only to find a moment later that he had to take them out again and feel through his pockets for a ten pence piece with which to close the locker and release the key. He pinned the key to his swimming costume, then, towel in hand, gave a wide berth to the eighty-year-old (now flailing about inside his shirt), and emerging into the corridor, turned left and followed the signs that said 'Stanhope Pool'.

After the preceding seediness, the pool itself was a pleasant surprise: a cube of enticing blue set like a jewel in a vast and vaulted room that boasted a raised gallery at the far end, a tracery of metal girders across the ceiling, and, on a chair against the opposite wall, a rather sexy little life-guard playing the mouth organ.

Ralph hung his towel on the row of hooks along the nearest wall and approached the edge of the pool. Apart from a knot of splashing children in the shallow end, there were no more than half a dozen swimmers churning their way up and down its length – for which, as he lowered himself gingerly into the water, Ralph was profoundly grateful. A text-book homosexual sired by a dominant mother and retiring father, he'd never been remotely sporty. As a boy he'd shied away from the playing field, preferring the quiet of the library to the hurly-burly of soccer, stamp collecting to cadets, and had come to think of exercise as inimical to his particular sensibilities.

Imagine, then, his amazement on finding himself welcomed rather than chilled by the water, and discovering that although he didn't attempt more than ten unhurried lengths, sticking to a rather cautious breast stroke lest he collide with the other swimmers, he could emerge from the pool a quarter of an hour later feeling invigorated and refreshed.

Back in the changing room, he opened his locker, retrieved his clothes and began to towel himself dry. He was just slipping into his trousers when he heard the swing doors open, and looking up, saw a young man, towel strung negligently across his hips, make his way to the locker opposite. The young man had a bar of soap and a bottle of shampoo in his hands, which he placed on the seat next to Ralph before removing his towel and beginning to draw it vigorously back and forth across his back.

Trying his best not to let his eyes stray too obviously in the direction of the young man's body, Ralph sat down and felt for his shoes. A wave not exactly of lust, but more accurately of lust and sadness combined, engulfed him, and in his mind's eye he was taken back to his swimming classes at school and the sight of Mr Eedes, his swimming master, pulling on his trunks and heedlessly tucking what the other boys sniggeringly called his tackle into its pouch of clinging nylon.

'You got the time?'

'I beg your pardon?' Startled out of his reverie, Ralph instantly, and hotly, began to blush.

'The time,' repeated the young man. 'You got the time?'

'I'm sorry. The time. Yes, of course.' Ralph fumbled with the cuff of his shirt and consulted his watch. 'Just gone eleven.'

'Eleven. Right.' The young man had finished drying, and now he stretched languidly, throwing back his arms and pulling in his stomach, so that his cock, surmounted by its dense bush of hair, hung proud of his muscular legs.

This time Ralph was unable to tear away his eyes, and when the young man looked down again, it was directly into the older man's gaze. He let his hand fall to his cock, and with a slow, knowing smile, said: 'I always swim mid-morning. It's quieter then. Later you get the schoolkids, and at lunchtime the businessmen.'

'I suppose,' said Ralph. 'Of course. That would make sense.'

'And in the evenings,' continued the young man, 'you can hardly move in there.' He had a faint stubble, and his hair, curly on top, was cut short at the sides.

'I really wouldn't know.' Ralph forced himself upright and began folding his swimming costume into his towel. 'This is my first time.'

The young man's hand was lightly caressing his stomach. 'Good exercise,' he said. 'Swimming. The best.'

Ralph cleared his throat and pointed at the young man's soap. 'Tell me. Is there a shower?'

Again the young man smiled, and again there was, in his smile, a hint of teasing, taunting complicity. 'Sure,' he said. 'At the far end of the baths. Under the gallery.'

Then, turning his back on Ralph, he opened his locker and pulled out a pair of expensive-looking boxer shorts.

Back at the flat, Ralph dropped his towel on the table, collapsed on to his sofa bed and had to wait a good ten minutes before his excitement subsided. Then, going through to the kitchen, he put on the kettle, made himself a cup of coffee, and took it into the living-room.

He'd bought the flat in the early eighties. Although tiny, consisting merely of a living-room that doubled as bedroom, a galley kitchen, a bathroom and toilet, he had, with the help of John, who was an interior decorator, made it so stylish that visitors never noticed its size. The bathroom they'd painted an opulent maroon, the kitchen they'd done in lemon and white, and in the living-room the functional furniture was offset by dove grey walls and curtains of the palest mauve.

Sometimes Ralph wished the flat looked more homely, that there was a touch of chintz somewhere, a battered old chair, or that he wasn't quite so obsessive about keeping it clean. But that wasn't in his nature, and it had to be said that no matter who visited the flat, be they friend or one-night stand, it was always, and extravagantly admired, even down to the last of his carefully chosen ornaments.

Only his mother expressed reservations – but then there was nothing about his life of which she did approve, and never had, ever since George.

He took his coffee to the window, and with the image of the young man from the baths flickering in a recess of his mind, thought back across eighteen years to the madness of those two months with George. Just twenty-two, he'd been in his final year of college and living in a bedsit in Kennington. He could no longer remember exactly where he had been, but it was returning from some party or other at one in the morning that he'd seen, coming towards him along Kennington Lane, a sheer Adonis, a blond and fiery god, who'd caught his eye as they passed, looked over his shoulder at the same moment Ralph had done, and lingered at the next corner, exactly like Ralph, the one a mirror image of the other, both wanting . . .

Ralph sighed. He knew what he'd wanted. He'd wanted that beauty, that perfection, and the promise it held of reciprocity. But George? George, it transpired, had wanted only the mirror that Ralph held up to his beauty. 'All the better,' as Ralph had spat at his departing back, 'to admire yourself in.' Oh, he'd gone along with Ralph, allowed Ralph to make plans for the two of them, moved in, even, for a couple of weeks, but it had all been a dream, an illusion, that most predictable of traps set for the lonely, a fantasy. George was in love with love, and when Ralph's love proved altogether too constant, too reassuring, George had, of course, shrugged him off and gone in search of other, more arbitrary, and therefore more stimulating loves.

And Ralph? Ralph had been left to pick up the pieces and cry, literally cry, for two solid weeks, until John and Henry, bored by this excess of grief, had dragged him to Mykonos and arranged one night for a young Greek to wait in his room so that when the three of them got back from their night on the town, there he was, this Greek, this other, lesser god, spread-eagled on his bed.

Except that not even then had Ralph got over George, not properly, nor the awful thing that George had taught him, that love between men was, by its very nature, transitory. Nor, and here a bitter smile played about his lips, would he ever get over that other legacy of his weeks with George, the loss of his mother's love. For when George had moved into his bedsit in Kennington, so certain was Ralph that this was forever that he'd gone joyfully, gaily to see his mother and tell her he was, in every sense of the word, gay. Except that wasn't the word he'd used. He'd used her terminology: queer.

Nothing in his relationship with his mother, who'd always been so proud of him, so certain he was marked for something special, had prepared him for the vitriol she loosed on him that weekend. After the tears and hysteria, after the 'What have I done to deserve this?' and the 'Where did I go wrong?' came the 'I've read about your sort. It's dirty and unnatural. You're fooling yourself if you think it can last.'

He'd protested, of course, told her he wasn't like that, that he and George were going to live together for ever, just like a married couple, and that anyway, it wasn't something he had any control over, he'd always been like that, ever since – and here he made the mistake of telling her how Mr Eedes' body had branded itself on his adolescent consciousness, pointing the way forward. Then she'd really given way to her horror, and lunging at him across the room, had ordered him out of the house.

Of course she loved him really, he knew that, just as he loved her, and eventually they'd started spending Christmases together again, and even gone motoring in the Lake District the year before last. But it wasn't the same. Her disapproval hung over everything they did, although now it no longer manifested itself over his sexuality – that, as a subject, was taboo – but opted instead for the size of his flat, the fact that he wasn't making enough of himself, that she couldn't for the life of her understand why he'd given up his studies to become, of all things, a butler.

He brushed away the tear that had formed in his eye. What he could never tell his mother was that if she hadn't reacted as she had to the news of his sexuality, then perhaps he would have continued his studies. But when, the week after his mother's attack, George had announced he didn't want to cope with Ralph's emotional baggage or be dragged into his relationship with his mother, that wasn't what being gay was about, for that you might as well be heterosexual, Ralph had started to neglect his work, and when, at the end of the year, he'd failed his finals, what option had he had, when you looked at it, except to run away, to start travelling, in search not just of places where he wasn't known and could therefore be himself, but of the boys who were to be found in those places, in the bars and on the beaches of Greece and Italy, the Caribbean and South America? Not that it did to knock his years of travel. They'd taught him all he knew about serving others, not only as a waiter and butler, but also – and here he smiled crookedly – as celebrant of the male form.

He finished his coffee and taking his cup into the kitchen, washed it and put it back in the cupboard. One shouldn't complain. So what if he hadn't planned on becoming a butler? It gave him a reasonable living, and besides, he had fast friends in John and Henry, not to mention Claire from across the road, who, when it did get to him occasionally that there'd never been another George, would invite him into the post-feminist chaos of her flat and console him with her own accounts of the horrors to be suffered at the hands of a man.

And as of today, going hand in hand with the promise of a trimmer body from the swimming, as of today there was this youngster from the pool, fine fodder – what finer? – for fantasy. Again Ralph smiled. By now George would doubtless be fat or balding or both, and he'd always left a lot to be desired in the cock department. The boy from the pool, with his muscular legs, his inviting smile and neat little ears, the boy from the pool was as close to perfection as it was possible to come. More, reflected Ralph, at the age of forty and after only one visit to the baths, it would be indecent to expect.

That night he had a dinner in Mayfair for Lord Cartwright, one of his more demanding regulars, and he didn't get home till after two. He made sure, though, to set his alarm for nine. He wanted to bath and shave before his swim so that he was looking his best when he put in his second appearance at the baths.

He entered the foyer at ten forty sharp, and knew when he got to the changing room that he'd timed things perfectly. There at the bench was the eighty-year-old, struggling into his underpants. Ralph made for the locker he'd used the day before, and as he began to undo his buttons, noticed with surprise that his hands were trembling, and that the sensation in his stomach echoed the sensation of all those years before, when he'd stood on Kennington Lane looking back to his Adonis on the corner. 'Ah,' he could hear John murmur. 'L'amour, l'amour!' Without bothering to fold his clothes, he bundled them into his locker and fumblingly retrieved the key.

At the poolside, he scoured the handful of swimmers to see if he could pick out the boy. It was, though, impossible. His could have been any one of the submerged, churning bodies. So, slipping in at the deep end, Ralph forced himself to concentrate on his breast stroke; and found, to his surprise, that the swimming so calmed him that his stomach had returned to normal by the time he emerged from the pool and made for the door under the gallery marked MEN.

The showers were empty, and something of a shock after the pool. If the changing rooms were shabby, the showers were worse. The paint hung in unsightly strips from the ceiling, there was mould on the walls, and on the floor in the corners of the room, under the blue plastic matting, accretions of hair and soggy paper. Not, thought Ralph shuddering, an ideal setting for seduction.

Picking his way across the mat, he chose the shower by the window, and stepping under its torrent, slipped out of his swimming costume.

· He lost count of the time he stood under the shower, but when, quite superfluously, he'd finished soaping himself for the third or fourth time, and was still alone, it dawned on him that maybe the boy, knowing that he hadn't showered yesterday, had skipped the shower himself, hoping to meet Ralph in the changing room – and without losing another minute, he switched off the water, snatched up his towel and ran for the door.

A burst of noise greeted him as he approached the changing room, and pushing open the swing door, he found himself besieged by a throng of shouting, screaming schoolboys. A weary master, too weary to return Ralph's startled nod of greeting, stood by the wall, every so often barking at the more rowdy of their number to keep the noise down. No sign, though, of the young man.

Miserably, Ralph fought through the boys to his locker, and facing into the corner, began swiftly to dress.

It was the same the next day, and the next, no sign at all of the young man, and on both occasions the gauntlet to run of a dizzying horde of schoolchildren who, when they weren't stealing each other's towels, or reporting each other to their master for swearing, would stare pointedly at Ralph before dissolving into gales of laughter.

He began to wonder if he should give up the swimming, and then, more sensibly, decided to give up his fantasies about the young man. The swimming was good for him – better, certainly, than any fantasy – and given the state of his body, he owed it to himself to concentrate on doing that extra length each day, so that by the end of the week he would be up to fifteen and a good deal less puffed when he emerged from the pool.

So, in his mother's phrase, he knuckled to, managing by the Thursday, and not too breathlessly, to complete his target of fourteen lengths. Except that he hadn't, of course, forgotten so much as a follicle of his fantasy – and when, on the Friday, the shower door swung open, and through it, as stunning in the flesh as in memory, came the young man, Ralph realized that powering his every length up and down the pool had been the hope that the young man would, as he was doing now, materialize again, and pausing on the threshold to close the door behind him, step under the shower next to Ralph's and slip off his trunks. Ralph waited for his breathing to return to normal. Then, not daring to catch the young man's eye, he retrieved his soap from its container and began very carefully to lather himself a second time.

'Do you mind if I borrow some shampoo?'

Ralph looked up and found himself confronted by that remembered, knowing smile.

'Of course. Here.' And fumbling behind him on the windowsill, he handed the young man his shampoo.

The young man poured a generous dollop of shampoo into the palm of his hand and returned the bottle to Ralph.

'You haven't been swimming,' said Ralph. 'Since the last time.'

'No,' said the young man. 'Work.'

'Been busy, then?'

The young man nodded.

'What do you do?'

'I'm a writer.'

'A writer? Really?'

Again the young man nodded.

'Books?'

'Scripts.'

The young man closed his eyes and began to lather his hair. His body was angled towards Ralph, and as he worked at his hair, his eyes still closed, Ralph was able to devour its every detail. He felt himself starting to harden and turned away.

'And anyway,' he heard the young man say, 'you sometimes get the schoolkids on Wednesday and Thursday. Nasty brats.'

'Don't tell me. Noisy lot.'

'Exactly.'

Unable to look away any longer, Ralph once again turned to face his fantasy. Cock in hand, the young man was lathering between his legs. He looked up and saw the direction of Ralph's gaze, then looked down and saw the extent of Ralph's excitement. His eyes went hard, and twisting sideways, he muttered something under his breath.

For a moment Ralph couldn't think what to do next; then, his panic subsiding, he decided it would only compound matters if he didn't acknowledge the mutter.

'I'm sorry,' he said faintly. 'I didn't hear.'

The young man swung round. 'I said it's a good thing you've got a towel. You're going to need it.' And with those hard, ungiving eyes, he held Ralph's gaze until Ralph, near to fainting, snatched up the aforementioned article, and shielding himself behind it, fled from the showers.

For the next three days Ralph didn't go to the baths at all. He was simply too frightened; too frightened and too hurt. Never in his life had he made such a fool of himself. Then, as rationality returned, and because Claire stopped him in the street to say how well he was looking now that he'd started swimming, he took a deep breath and set out once more.

After all, it wasn't as if this was the first time he'd been given the brush-off, nor was it likely the young man would report him to the pool authorities. No, as long as in future he avoided the young man's eyes, no harm – no lasting harm, that is – had been done. He'd even been made to relearn a valuable lesson: that if he wanted a man, well, the trick was to keep it simple, as simple as the tricks themselves, and to hunt for them only in the clubs, where the manner in which they displayed themselves wasn't open to misinterpretation.

He was relieved to find, as he entered the changing

room, that the young man wasn't there – nor, for once, the perennial eighty-year-old – and it was with a light, determined step that he crossed to locker 40 and began to undress. He'd only got as far, however, as slipping off his shoes, when another young man came swinging into the room, a young man every bit as heart-stopping as the first. For a moment, despite himself, Ralph gasped: gasped and was tempted to gawk. But he'd learnt his lesson, and even when the young man commented on what a nice day it was, Ralph kept his head averted. He couldn't, of course, help a quick sideways glance as the young man peeled down his jeans, but no sooner had he seen what he wanted to see than he looked away again, and scooping up his soap and shampoo, made for the pool.

There, pacing himself carefully, and emptying his mind of thought, he managed to swim as many as twenty lengths, and one for luck, before getting out and making for the shower. To his amazement (for he'd still been ostentatiously naked when Ralph had left the changing room) the young man was there before him, under the shower by the window. Ralph opted for the shower in the opposite corner, balanced his soap on the tap and began, with particular absorption, to wash himself.

It was some moments before he looked up again to discover that the young man was staring at him.

'Knackering, huh?' The young man's eyes were decidedly mischievous, and that wasn't all: his hand was making another kind of mischief with what hung between his legs.

Ralph turned quickly away and reached for his soap.

A second later, and much to his relief, he heard the door open, though when he glanced up to see who it was, he found to his horror that he was looking straight into the taunting eyes of the very man he'd been avoiding. His first instinct was to bolt, but something – he didn't know what – made him hold back, hold back and watch with growing amazement as, stepping casually under the shower midway between Ralph and the first young man, the newcomer slipped off his trunks, and taking out his soap, began with slow, luxurious strokes to apply it to his cock. Unable now to tear his eyes away, Ralph watched mesmerized as both young men began to soap themselves until their cocks came wholly erect. Then, shooting a look half of defiance, half of disdain at Ralph, the young man nearest to him leant over and reached for the other man's cock. It didn't take the pair of them more than a minute to come. Then, as if nothing more untoward had happened than an exchange of shampoo or a request for the time, both men returned to their separate ablutions. Ralph looked down at his own, pathetically eager member, and powerless to prevent himself, came on the spot in a series of short, sharp spurts.

'No kids today,' said the young man in the middle.

Ralph, in the panicked process of gathering up his things and preparing to leave, was forced to hesitate. 'I beg your pardon?'

'No kids,' repeated the young man, fixing him with a look of quite devastating neutrality.

'No, indeed,' stuttered Ralph. 'No kids.'

'Yeah, don't you hate those fucking kids,' supplied the other young man. 'Really hate them.'

That night, at the club, Ralph confided in John and Henry.

'I mean,' he said, 'isn't it bizarre? What is he playing at?'

'What young men like to play at,' said John. 'Each other.'

'But why lead me on like that? He flirts with me, then he cuts me dead, then he comes in front of me.'

'Narcissism, dear,' said Henry. 'Young men like that get a kick out of being admired. I should know. I've done enough admiring in my time to satisfy whole armies of them.'

'No,' said Ralph, 'it's more than that.'

'Oh really?' said Henry. 'In what way?'

'I don't know. Something in me, perhaps. Some reaction I invite.'

'If you want a partner,' said John, 'don't go looking in the locker rooms of London. Ring a dating agency.'

'Who said I wanted a partner?'

'Sorry, I could have sworn you did.'

He hadn't, of course, he'd never confided that to anyone, not even Claire. But John had been right. He did want a partner, it was what he'd always wanted, and always would – except, and this was the problem, his partner had to be a man, and men weren't made for permanence.

He didn't go swimming for a week after that, and when he took it up again, it was first thing in the morning, when the pool was full of commuters on their way to work, men in hock to their mortgages and their marriages who, if they noticed Ralph at all, took him as one of their own.

And then, when he was least expecting it, he met the young man again – not at the pool, but at Mrs Bartholomew's. Mrs Bartholomew was married to a financier, and every couple of months she held a dinner, either to oil the wheels of her husband's current deal, or else, more frivolously, to flaunt some media personality before her friends. On this occasion her find was an elderly American film star who'd been rescued from obscurity and a more or less permanent suite at the Betty Ford Clinic by a triumphant revival, first seen on Broadway and now transferring to Shaftesbury Avenue, of a Kaufman classic written as a vehicle for the star's mother.

'Ralph, angel!' Mrs Bartholomew had cooed when she'd phoned to book him. 'I want to push the boat out.

You know Americans. They love a touch of the Jeeves. As formal as you can make it, yes? Let's give the old has-been the works.'

It was, accordingly, a Ralph as crisp as his wing collar who marched to the door on the third or fourth ring, and throwing it open, saw at first glance a man in a white linen suit, all twined about by a dark-haired beauty in a sheath of red, and then, on closer inspection, seeing through the social disguise at the same moment as the young man penetrated his, recognized the eyes.

Keeping his voice level only by the most mammoth effort, Ralph stepped back from the door and said: 'Good evening, sir. Madam. Who shall I say?'

Charmed by this apparition from a bygone age, the woman whispered something in the young man's ear. The young man, however, didn't take his eyes from Ralph's as he drew his partner across the threshold and replied, in a voice every bit as level: 'Mr and Mrs Parker.'

'Just a minute!' The woman flashed Ralph a winning smile, and turning to the mirror on the wall, began fussing expertly with her luxuriant tumble of auburn curls.

Ralph closed the door, and without daring to glance again at either of them, led the way to the drawing-room and made the announcement: 'Mr and Mrs Parker.' In an instant, Mrs Bartholomew, in a swirl of unsuitable pink, was upon them, and with a cry of 'Laura, my dear, and Charles, how well you both look!' hustled them off to meet the film star, who'd been propped, like a piece of statuary, against the fireplace.

If he could have left then, he would have – but although he'd become a butler by chance (in spite of himself, and perhaps, also, to spite himself) Ralph had over the years come to take a certain pride in his work. So, drawing himself up to his full height, he returned stiffly to the hallway to await the next guests.

He didn't see his nemesis again until dinner, when, much to his discomfort, far from avoiding his eye, the young man seemed to lose no opportunity in catching it and allowing a flicker of amused recognition to play about his lips.

Then, after the main course, and as Ralph was clearing the dishes, the young man caught him by the sleeve and whispered in his ear: 'I'm absolutely bursting. Can you show me where it is?'

Instinctively, Ralph shot a look across the table to the young man's wife. Mercifully, she was deep in conversation with the man on her left.

'Of course, sir,' he said. 'If you'll follow me.' And pulling back the young man's chair, he ushered him from the room.

'Heavy duty stuff, eh?' smiled the young man as they reached the hallway. 'Old Amy certainly knows how to lay it on.'

Ralph didn't pause in his progress towards the passage that led to the downstairs loo.

'Don't look so bloody uncomfortable,' said the young man. 'I won't tell if you won't.'

Whereupon, to his horror, Ralph felt a hand on his thigh.

'Here it is, sir,' he said. 'Through that door there.' And averting his eyes, he stepped aside to let the young man pass.

'In here, you say?' The young man opened the door and stepped into the loo.

Ralph made to turn away, but he wasn't quick enough. No sooner had the young man slipped inside the loo than, already erect, he had his cock out.

'Come on,' he whispered. 'It won't take a minute.'

'I really think, sir,' began Ralph – and then, drawing himself up: 'I really must be getting back.'

The young man merely ran his hand with enticing deftness up and down the length of his shaft.

'Come on,' he said again. 'I know you want to.' And hitching up his shirt, he revealed a wedge of hard, flat stomach.

Surprising himself with the force with which he uttered the words, Ralph put a finger inside his wing collar to loosen its stranglehold on his neck and said: 'I'm sorry. You had your chance.'

The young man let go of his cock and his eyes went hard.

'I beg your pardon?'

'I think you heard.'

'But isn't this what butlers do? Serve?'

'Some butlers, maybe,' said Ralph. 'Not this one.'

And swivelling sharply, he retraced his footsteps down the passage. When he reached the safety of the hallway, he turned, and saw that although the young man had at least had the grace to put away his cock, he was still standing in the open doorway of the loo. He looked almost exactly as George had looked, standing on the corner of Kennington Lane all those years ago, and it came to Ralph suddenly that what had been wrong between George and him was not, as his mother had said, that it was two men, and therefore transitory, but that they had made it so. For although George had been in love primarily with love, and with any admiration of his body, what Ralph hadn't realized till now was that all he had been able to offer George in return was precisely that: adoration. It wasn't enough to hold up a mirror to another, or to ask them to hold up a mirror to you. True love happened only when the mirror was smashed and together you stepped through it to the other side.

'Sir has a most beautiful body,' he said stiffly. 'But even so, I think sir would be better served by that.'

And gesturing to the rococo mirror which hung on the passage wall, and in which sir was reflected, so that if you removed Ralph from the scene, it would have seemed as if the young man was coming on to himself, Ralph returned to the dining-room, where Mrs Bartholomew, beckoning him to her seat at the head of the table, said: 'Thank heavens, Ralph. For a moment there I thought we'd lost you. Dessert, I think.' And as he turned away to organize it, caught him by the arm and murmured in tones of extravagant but genuine appreciation: 'Tonight, Ralph, you've excelled yourself. You really are the most splendid of butlers. I don't know what we'd do without you.'

Incubus

*or The Impossibility of
Self-Determination as to Desire*

WILL SELF

June Laughton, a prize-winning gardener and Peter Geddes, her husband, a philosopher no less, were having an altercation in the kitchen of their ugly house.

The house was indubitably ugly but it had an interesting feature which meant that English Heritage paid for its maintenance and upkeep. The altercation was on the verge of getting ugly – although not quite so ugly as the house. It concerned Peter Geddes's habit of employing the very tip of his little finger as a spatula with which to scoop out the fine, white rheum from the corners of his pink eyes. This he transferred to his moist mouth, again and again. Each fingerful was so Lilliputian a repast that he required constant refreshment.

It was one of those aspects of her husband that June Laughton could stomach on a good day – but only on a good day.

'It's disgusting . . .' she expostulated.

'. . . I can't help it,' he retorted. 'It's a compulsion.'

'Don't be stupid. How can something like that be a compulsion?'

'Oh, all right – I don't mean compulsion. I mean that it's an involuntary action, I don't have any control over it.'

'Sometimes I think that you don't have any control over anything,' and she banged the egg-encrusted frying pan into the sink to give her judgement proper emphasis.

The action was a failure. Her husband didn't pay any attention and the frying pan broke a glass. A glass dirtied with stale whisky, that was lingering in the bottom of the aluminium trough. Naturally it was June who had to pick the fragments out, extract them from the slurry of food fragments and cutlery that loitered around the plug hole.

'Of course, strictly speaking you could be right about that . . . Mmm.' Peter's head was bent as he fiddled on the table top.

'Ouch!' June registered intense irritation and intense pain simultaneously: her husband's edifying tone lancing up under her fingernail alongside a sliver of glass from the broken vessel. 'Why can't you do your own washing up? Look what you've done to me.' She turned from the sink to face him, holding up her wounded paw, fingers outstretched.

Peter Geddes regarded his wife and thought, 'How like the Madonna she is, or Marcel's description of the Duchesse de Guermantes, the first time he sees her in the church at Combray.' He had a point, June Laughton was formidably beautiful. Behind her face bone tented flesh into pure arabesque. Her neck was long and undulant. So long that she could never hold her head straight. It was always at an angle, capturing whatever wash of prettifying light was on offer. Now, in this particular pose, with her hand spread, red rivulet running down her index finger, she was even beatified by the commonplace.

'But darling, that's what Giselle is for, in part at any rate. She'll do all the washing up.'

'Don't be absurd Peter. You can't expect a research assistant to labour at your turgid book all day and do domestic service as well . . .'

'. . . That's what she's for. That's what she's offered to do. Look, I know you find it very difficult to believe but I'm actually well thought of, respected, in what I do – '

' – What's that you're doing now?'

'What?'

'You're writing on the table. You're writing on the bloody table! I suppose you're going to tell me that's an involuntary action as well.'

'What this, this? H-hn, h-hn-hn, ha-hn.' He went into his affected, fat man's chortle. 'Oh no, no no. No this is a truth table. A truth table as it were on a truth table. H-hn h-hn, insofar as when we sit at this table we attempt to tell the truth. And this, this . . .' he gestured at the square grid of letters and symbols that he had inscribed on the formica surface, '. . . is a truth table expressing the necessary and sufficient conditions of an action being intentional, being willed. Do you want me to explain it further old girl?'

'No I don't. I want you out of here. And that girl, research assistant, au pair, factotum or scullery maid. Whatever she is – you'll have to pick her up from Grantham yourself in the Renault. Unless you've forgotten, the twins get back today.'

'No I hadn't forgotten. How long will they be here for?'

'A week or two, and then they're off to Burgundy for the grape picking.'

'Together?'

'Of course.'

They cracked up in the synchronized spasm that only comes after souls have been engrafted, bonded by white rheum, cemented by dusty semen, glued by the placenta. The funniest thing in their lives was their children, the non-identical twins, the girl tall and opulently beautiful like her mother, the boy, short, fat, cardigan-cuddly like his dear old buffer-dad.

The twins' inseparability had resisted all their parents' attempts to drive them apart, to wedge them into individuality. When they came home together, from their university, or their predictable travels – inter-railing, inefficiently

digging irrigation ditches for peasants, offending
Muslims – their parents laughed again at the funhouse
image of their young selves incestuously bonded.

'Had you thought of putting them in the Rood Room?'
Peter flung this over his shoulder as he worked his way
round the awkward curved corridor that led from the
kitchen to the rest of the house.

'Oh no, your Giselle must have the Rood Room. After
all she has to have some compensation for becoming an
indentured serf.'

Later that day Peter Geddes waited in his car for Giselle
to exit from Grantham station. There were never many
passengers on this mid-afternoon stopper from Liverpool
Street so he knew he wouldn't miss her. Despite this he
adopted a sort of sit-up-and-beg posture in the hard, functional seat of the car, as if he were a private detective waiting to follow a suspect. He did this because he had the
heightened self-consciousness of an intelligent person
who has drunk slightly too much alcohol in the middle of
the day.

'Sorry,' said Giselle, coming up on Peter unawares and
hallooing in the characteristic manner of an English bourgeois.

'Whossat!' He started.

'Sorry,' she reiterated. 'I was late and got stuck in the
rear carriage. It's taken me ages to lug this lot up the plat-
form. I couldn't find a porter or anyone.'

It didn't occur to Peter to cancel out her superfluous
apology with one more justified. But he did get out and
load her luggage through the back hatch. There was a lot
of it. Two scuffed, functional suitcases, two straw baskets
which wafted pot pourri, a rolled Peruvian blanket and
so on.

They drove through Grantham. A plump man and a

plump girl. Both philosophers and therefore necessarily free in spirit, yet still mundanely hobbled by avoirdupois, like battery porkers being fattened up to do metaphysics. Peter spoke first. 'It's a dull little town, we hardly bother to come in here. You can get just about everything you need in Bumford.'

'Is your house right in the village?'

'No, it's on the outskirts, on the Vale of Belvoir side.'

'Oh, that must be lovely.'

'No, not exactly. You'll see what I mean.'

She did. The town of Grantham gave way to the unmade, unfinished countryside of South Notts. The scrappy alternation of light industry and industrial farming gave the area a sort of kitchen-where-no-one-has-washed-up feeling. The Vale of Belvoir, which was the only feature for miles around, was little more than a yellow, rape-filled runnel, spreading out towards a hazy horizon, giving the distinct impression that all of England was a desultory plateau, falling away to the north.

'Well Giselle, this is your home for the foreseeable future, or at least until we can get this bloody book finished.' Peter abruptly braked the Renault, scrunching the gravel. They sat for a moment, still in the monochrome of a dull summer afternoon, listening to an electric mower and each other's breathing. Even Giselle couldn't summon up much more of a comment about the house than: 'Ooh, how interesting. It must have been quite unique when it was built.' As good an example of the enigma of the counterfactual as any.

Peter took her inside. June was off getting the twins from Stansted. He led her through the cramped rooms on the ground floor and up the back stairs. They entered the Rood Room.

'My golly!' cried Giselle. 'I don't think I've ever seen anything like this before. How? I mean what . . .?'

'. . . Yes, yes, well, the Rood Room often does take people this way. I'll give you the edited lecture, then if you want to know more you can read the pamphlet English Heritage have done on it.'

'Is this . . .?'

'. . . Where you'll be sleeping, yes, that is if you think you can cope with it?'

'Cope with it, why, it's beautiful.'

'Perhaps that's putting it a bit strongly but it is an unusual room, a characterful room.

'It was built by a local craftsman called Peter Horner, in the mid seventeenth century. As you can see, the room is dominated by an outsize version of a traditional rood screen. Originally this feature would have separated the nave of the church from the choir and been surmounted by a crucifix. Its status as a symbolic dividing of the congregation from the priest is obvious, but here in the Rood Room the symbolism of the screen has been subverted.

'Horner was a member of a local Manichean sect called the Grunters. He probably built the room as a secret worshipping place for the sect. The screen itself, instead of being topped by a crucifix, is capped by a number of phalluses. Some of these descend from the ceiling, like plaster stalactites, some ascend from the screen like wooden stalagmites. The overall effect is rather toothy, wouldn't you say?'

'It's astonishing. And all carving, painting and plasterwork. It's all so fresh and vivid.'

'Yes, well, of course the Rood Room has been extensively restored. As a matter of fact by a team of unemployed architectural graduates working under the direction of our own dear Dr Morrison. Nevertheless it was remarkably preserved to begin with. It is without doubt the foremost example of seventeenth century vernacular architecture still extant in England.'

'Actually Dr Geddes, it does seem odd . . . I mean not that I don't want to . . . but sleeping in a place of worship . . .'

'. . . Oh I shouldn't give it another thought. We've been living here for years, since the twins were small and they always slept here. And anyway, you have to consider what the Grunters' probable form of worship was. Like other Manicheans they believed that as the Devil was coeternal with God, forms of behaviour that orthodox Christians regarded as sinful were in fact to be enjoined. Hence all these rude, rather than "rood", paintings and carvings.'

Giselle fell to examining the panels of the rood screen and Peter, remembering his more material duties as host and employer, went off to fetch her cases from the car.

Standing in front of the house Peter looked up at its façade and shook his head in weary enjoyment. 'It never fails,' he thought, 'it never fails to surprise them.' Had he troubled to analyse his glee at exposing the Rood Room to Giselle, he might have found it to be a more complicated and troublesome emotion. After all, shocking guests with the Rood Room was akin to a sophisticated form of flashing.

Because the exterior of the Geddes–Laughton house was so uncompromisingly Victorian – two shoeboxes of dark red London brick, topped off with a steeply gabled tile roof – any visitor was bound to expect its interior to correspond. But it was only a cladding, a long mackintosh that could be twitched aside to reveal a priapic core. For really the house was a collection of seventeenth-century cottages and hovels that had been cemented together over the centuries by a mucilage of plaster, wattle, daub and stonework. The only room of any substance was the Rood Room, all the others were awkward moulded cells, connected by bulging, serpentine corridors.

But Peter didn't trouble to analyse his emotions – it wasn't his style. It's difficult to imagine what the interior scape of a philosopher's mind might be like. Modern works of analytic philosophy are so arid. How could anyone hold so many fiddly Fabergé arguments in his or her mind for so long? Without the drifting motes of decaying brain cells – used up thoughts and prototypical thoughts never to be employed – beginning to fill the atmosphere and cloud the clarity of introspection with intellectual plaster dust.

To get around the problem, Peter's mind was akilter to real time. Like a gyroscope spinning slowly, set inside another gyroscope spinning faster, Peter's mind went on churning through chains, puzzles and tables of ratiocination, while the world zipped by him: a time-lapse film with a soundtrack of piping, irrelevant Pinky and Perky voices. And while not exactly fecund, the similes required to describe his mental processes are sterile rather than decaying. These mind manipulations were like three-dimensional word puzzles: propositions, premises, theses and antitheses, all in free fall, coaxed into place with a definite 'click'. It was as if Peter's will were a robotic claw, that lanced into a radioactive interior in order to perform subtle experiments.

But then the greatest paradox of all is that nothing is farther from self-knowledge than introspection, and nothing more remote from wisdom than pure intellect.

On re-entering the house, Peter found Giselle in the kitchen. She was arranging some freesias in a jam jar full of water as he popped puffing through the narrow door.

'You must let me help you with those, they're awfully heavy.'

'Oh no – no. Don't worry. You sit down. Bung on the kettle if you like.' He was already mounting the awkward steps.

Back upstairs he placed her cases and baskets by the big

pine bedstead set beneath the largest window. He sat on the edge of the bed and lost himself for a while in the Rood Room's gullet confines.

It really was an astonishing place, hardly like a room in a house at all, more of a grotto. There was one large, diamond mullioned window over the bed and another, much smaller, on the opposite wall, the other side of the rood screen. The light from these came in in thick shafts, given body by swirls of golden dust motes. But it was the ceiling that gave the room its organic feel. It was thrown over the top like a counterpane. The middle of the billowing roof was held aloft, over the dead centre of the rood screen, supported there by its petrified folds. Between these folds, studding the rippling walls, were hundreds of plaster mouldings.

Running up from the room's corners to its apex were seams of lozenges entwined by ivy. But this simple decoration was nothing compared to the profusion of body parts – gargoyle heads, thrusting breasts, dangling penises; as well as a comprehensive bestiary, griffins and sphinxes, bulls rampant, lions couchant – that sprouted across the rest of the curved surfaces. The eye could not take in the whole of this decoration – there were over four hundred individual reliefs – instead it reduced them to a warty effect.

Each side of the rood screen itself was adorned with some thirteen individual painted panels. Dr Morrison may have assured English Heritage that his assistants had used authentic reformulations of the original pigments to retouch the screen, yet the result was advertisingly garish. The white and flat bodies of the Grunters lay entwined in naïve tableaux of sexual abandon. They sported in distorted copses of painful viridity and dug from the excremental earth the falsely dead cadavers of their brethren, dragging them back into the one and only world.

Peter Geddes couldn't bear to look at the rood screen for too long. When he and June had bought the house some fifteen years ago, the Rood Room had been impressive, but in grimy decay. The screen was blackened and the images faint. The stippling of explicit carvings covering the walls had been chipped and disfigured into insignificance.

Dr Morrison and his crew had only finished their restoration work that spring. Now, in the glory of mid-summer with the garden outside groaning in prefructive labour, the Rood Room had acquired a pregnant burnish. The walls bellied pink, the screen glared. Even Peter was susceptible to the rioting colour and the strange sensation of heretical worship, resonating down the ages. He wondered, idly, if the room might have an adverse psychological effect on his new research student.

This reverie was cut into by the sound of the family station wagon pulling up outside, and shortly after, the shouts of his teenage twins resounded through the house. He came back down the cramped stairway and found the four of them already at tea.

Peter wasn't fazed as the four sets of eyes swivelled towards him. He knew that in his family's eyes he cut a somewhat embarrassing figure. Not exactly a looker: his duck-egg body defied his clothes to assume recognizable forms. On him, trousers ceased to be bifurcated, shirts stopped being assemblies of linen planes and tubes; and shoes became hopelessly adrift – merely functional stops to his roly-poly body – wedged underneath, as if to prevent him from toppling over.

None of this mattered to Peter, for he was one of those men who had managed in adolescence to wilfully disregard his physical form – for good. So, he entered the kitchen unabashed and crying 'Here you are, you rude mechanicals!' he cupped the head of his daughter and drew her cheek to his lips, then did the same with his son.

Giselle, whose father's touch was nothing but wince-provoking, was struck by the fact that neither twin struggled to free themselves from this. Quite the reverse: they seemed to lean into his kiss.

'Well, and how were the Dinka?' Peter went on, sitting down at the head of the table and reaching for a cup of tea. 'Did they let you drink milk and blood? Did you learn their eighty-seven different words to express the shape of their cattle's horns?'

'We haven't been with the Dinka Dad,' said Hal, the son, 'we haven't even been in Africa . . .'

'. . . Oh, I see, not in Africa. Next you're going to tell me that you didn't even leave England.'

'We did leave England,' said Pixy, the daughter, 'but we went north rather than south. We've been at a rural development project, working with the Lapps in northern Sweden . . .'

'. . . Drinking reindeer pee. And we've learnt fifteen different words to express the shape of a reindeer's antlers.' Her brother finished the account for her.

Giselle was charmed by this demonstration of familial good humour. Cuddling, nicknames, banter, all were alien to the privet-lined precincts of her proper parents.

They ate lardy cake and drank a lot of tea. The sounds of the B road that ran through the village reached them but faintly, drowned out by the rising evening chorus of the birds.

'Well!' June exclaimed, 'I can't sit here for the rest of the day. For one thing I shan't have room for dinner. I don't know if you had forgotten Peter but Henry and Caitlin are coming this evening – '

' – Of course I hadn't. I've got some suitably caustic burgundy. It's just dying to climb right out of its bottles and scour that self-satisfied man's mind.'

'Of course darling. I'm going to get back to work now,

or I shan't be able to finish re-turfing that lawn before dusk.' June rubbed her hands on her trouser legs, as if she could already feel the peat on her palms. 'You twins can do the cooking. Christ knows you're better at it than I am.'

'Oh but Ma, we're jet-lagged,' they chorused.

'Nonsense. Lapland is, as we all know, due north of here.'

There was a brief groaning duet, but no further protest. The twins went off to inhabit their rooms. Giselle stood up and began to tidy away the tea things.

'Don't worry about that,' June called out from the front door, 'leave it for the twins.'

'Oh, ah, OK. Well,' she giggled nervously, 'what to do? Should we . . .? I mean I have some notes relating to Chapter Four. It's the rather technical stuff – you know, where you demolish the compatibilist arguments. If you'd like to . . .'

'. . . Ah no. Don't worry about that now,' Peter sighed, looking up from the cake corpse he was feeding on. 'Free will and determinism will still be incompatible come the morning. You just relax. Breathe in the country air. I have some correspondence to deal with that'll take me the rest of today.'

Giselle followed June into the garden. The older woman was already plying a long-handled spade, picking up the turfs from a neat pile and laying them out in rows on the brushed bare soil. Giselle, rather than disturb her, walked in the opposite direction.

June Laughton had transformed the half acre or so of conventional ground into a miniature world of landscaping. Prospects had been foreshortened, or artificially lengthened, by clever earthworks, reflective pools and the planting of the obscurer varieties of pampas grass. On hummocks and in little dells she had embedded subtropical flowers and shrubs, varieties that survive in the local climate.

Giselle wandered enchanted. Like a lot of intellectuals she felt herself to be hopelessly impractical. This was an affectation that she had wilfully fostered, rather than a true trait. It allowed her to view the physical (and therefore inferior) achievements of others with false modesty, as heroic acts, as if they were plucky spastics who had entered a marathon.

So deceived was she by the clever layout of the garden that Giselle was startled, on rounding a clump of flora, to come upon June.

'Oh sorry!' she barked, compounding her own surprise with June's. June dropped her spade.

'That's OK,' she said. 'Enjoying the evening?'

'Oh it's lovely, really lovely. And it's amazing what you've done with this garden. I don't think I've ever seen anything quite like it.'

'No, it's not exactly your traditional English garden, is it. For years Peter and I were stuck in England, he with his work and I with the twins. I was determined to bring something of the foreign and the exotic into our lives, so I created this garden.' June bent and picked up her turfing spade. She stood and turned to give Giselle her profile.

Standing there in her peat-dusted corduroys, with her gingham shirt unbuttoned to the warm roots of her breasts, her thick, blonde hair falling away in a drape from its hooking grips, June was like a William Morris Ceres, gesturing to the fruits of her labours.

For ten minutes she strolled the garden with Giselle, pointing out the individual plants and describing their properties. Her manner was so gracious, so unselfconscious that the younger woman felt entirely at ease.

Giselle had been terribly worried about coming to stay with Dr Geddes. She was too young to be able to divorce the potency of the mind from that of the body, and when, in his capacity as her post-graduate supervisor, Peter enthused over ideas, slinging out arguments like conceptual clays, Giselle had been seduced, and longed for his wet mouth to clamp on hers.

She thought them a good match, they could be cuddly together. This was a dream she had harboured, but she was far too ethical, too upstanding ever to imagine that anything would come of it. And anyway, she could tell that he didn't even regard her as belonging to the same species as himself. In his disinterested gaze she saw only zoological interest.

While June and the twins made dinner Giselle was parcelled off to have a bath. She sported in the tub. She laved herself and laved herself and laved herself. Working up lather after lather after lather, until when at last she stood, steaming on the mat, her skin smelt of nothing but lavender. Her personal, indefinable odour was eradicated, sluiced away.

Back in the Rood Room, Giselle unpacked. She interleaved her chemises, blouses, slips and underwear in the broad drawers of a large dresser. She placed her books on the footstool by the double bed, together with a candle, shaped and scented like an orange. With little touches such as these, the Rood Room soon began to seem to Giselle like her room. She had that ability as a person – to feel almost instantly at home simply by the application to a new place of a small coating of personal artefacts.

Giselle had a tea ceremony that completed her unpacking. It was part of her divine indwelling, her personal mythologizing. She primed the tiny spirit burner, lit it, set a diminutive kettle on its stand, and unpacked some translucent bowls from their tissue paper. Then she slipped a silk dressing gown over her round shoulders. All of this had a ritual quality, a sacerdotal rhythm.

Here in Peter Geddes's house, in the Rood Room, the whole tea ceremony took on a potent aura. The sun was sinking down and the thick beams of light that entered the room from the smaller western window were combed by the top of the rood screen. Carious shadows snaked across the quilt, and over Giselle's crossed thighs, where she sat in its dead centre, her bowl of tea cradled in her lap.

Giselle felt drugged by bath and tea, ready to abandon herself to the Rood Room, to become just another painted panel.

'Am I free?' she thought. 'That's what I'm here for: to consider that question in its widest and narrowest senses. But am I? Wouldn't it be an achingly reductive proposition for one who was truly un-free to even bother to consider the grounds of that un-freedom?' Giselle hunched further upright on the lumpy softness of the mattress.

Her features were pretty enough. She had a fine-bridged nose, long and flaring into *retroussé*. Her eyes were large and dark violet. The smallness of her brow was well disguised by her long pelt of hair, which, falling inwards to her collarbone, served also to flatter the fullness of her figure.

The irony was, that seated there on her round haunches, although Giselle may not have possessed the sort of freedom that implies full moral responsibility, she nonetheless had plenty of that very prosaic power: the power of fey sexual self-awareness.

Pixy came scuttling under the low lintel and into the Rood Room. She was free. Entirely free of the painful shyness Giselle remembered blustering her way through at that age.

'Ooh, what a clever little thing.' Pixy was fiddling with the copper kettle on its spirit lamp, tipping it this way and that so splashes of still steaming water fell on to the windowsill.

'Careful – ' said Giselle.

' – Don't worry,' snapped back Pixy, 'I won't break it.' She took a turn around the Rood Room, looking closely at the panels and the plaster reliefs. 'Don't mind me,' she threw out after a while. 'I always like to come up and check out the Rood Room after I've been away for a while – you don't mind do you?'

'No, no, of course . . .'

'So you're a philosopher like Daddy are you?'

'Hardly,' Giselle demurred. 'Your father is extremely eminent. He's very likely to get the Pelagian professorship next year, especially if this book is a success.'

'And that's what you're here for?'

'To help him with the book, yes. Dr Geddes is my postgraduate supervisor. He very kindly offered me a couple of months work, both helping him out and helping your mother around the house . . .'

'So you're not here to screw him then?'

'PhsssNo!' Giselle sprayed the quilt with oolong.

'Well, that's just as well,' Pixy was halfway out of the door, 'because Mum says that he's got so fat he's hardly capable any more . . .' While Giselle was still too stunned to frame a rejoinder Pixy poked her blonde head back under the lintel. '. . . The guests are here by the way. You'd better dress and come down.'

As she hurriedly dressed, Giselle put Pixy's behaviour down to precocity rather than conscious rudeness. The other possibility – that the girl had somehow sensed Giselle's desire – was too awful to contemplate.

In the drawing-room she found Peter Geddes and another man drinking whisky. 'Giselle Dawson,' said Peter gesturing at her, 'this is Henry Beckwood.' He gestured at the man, who was twitchily thin, sporting bifocals and wire wool hair. 'Henry, Giselle is my new research assistant. Giselle, Henry is big in plastics.'

'. . . And not much else besides,' said the man called Henry, offering Giselle his hand. Seeing that she looked perplexed he added, 'what Peter means is that I'm a polymer scientist.'

'D'you want a drop of coloured water then Giselle?' Peter was holding the bottle around its shoulders and thrusting it at her, as if it were a club with which he was going to beat her into sedation.

'Err . . . no, thank you.'

'If you want something else, some wine say, you'll find it in the kitchen, on the truth table.'

As she left the room Giselle could hear Peter explaining to Henry why he called it the truth table. She found Peter's manner disconcerting. The bottle of whisky had been half-empty, but she couldn't believe that the two of them had already drunk that much, it was only eight o'clock.

'Pissed already are they?' said June as Giselle came into the kitchen. 'I know it's only eight but once you get Peter and Henry together there's no stopping them, is there Caitlin?' Giselle saw that there was another woman in the kitchen. She was middle-aged but with the figure of a gamine. She had pretty little features and an uncomfortably sharp, trowel-like chin. Giselle proffered her hand.

'Hi, I'm Giselle Dawson.'

'And I'm Caitlin Beckwood – and that's the only straight statement you're likely to get out of me all evening. June d'you have a corkscrew, I'm sure Giselle is dying for a glass of wine, I know I am.'

Dinner was accorded a great success.

A success as far as the two couples were concerned perhaps, but Giselle felt distinctly sidelined. The older people took one end of the table and the twins consorted at the other. Giselle was stuck in the middle, faced with either having to force herself into the grown ups' conversation, which was raucous and full of shared illusions, references to a communal history, or else relapse into her teens and the kind of join-the-dots self-assertion and clumsily plotted intimacy that was still all too fresh from her days as an undergraduate.

She got up after courses to help June and the twins with the clearing, but each time she was shooed back down into her seat. Not even this form of ordinary intercourse was allowed her.

It wasn't anything intentional on anyone's part – she knew that. It was just that the two older women had a lot to talk about – and so it seemed did the men. As for the twins, their communication consisted almost entirely of near-telepathic nods and lid dips, betokening leisured centres of self but thinly partitioned off from one another.

Giselle was struck by the way that neither of the men offered to assist in any way. Caitlin Beckwood had got up to do a late whip of the syllabub because she was 'good at that sort of thing', but the only contribution Peter made throughout the evening was to open bottle after bottle of the caustic burgundy, and the only contribution Henry made was to drink them. By the time the cheese board was passed round, the plot of the table that lay between them had been overdeveloped with empty bottles. They stood about like glass missile silos that had already shot their wad.

The wine had got to Peter and Henry's faces. It was particularly remarkable in Peter's case because he was wearing an intense, burgundy-coloured smoking jacket with quilted lapels. His white shirt was a wedge of light between the two blobs of vinous darkness.

It looked ridiculous, this posh bit of plush cast over his teddy-bear torso, and Peter seemed to regard it accordingly as a joke prop, occasionally flicking invisible particles of dust from the cuffs, as if punctuating his interminable philosophical wrangles with Henry by alluding to the insubstantiality of matter itself.

Throughout dinner, and even when they moved next door to have coffee and After Eights, they had talked Free Will. This was capitalized – in Giselle's mind – because so intense were their clashes that they might have been arguing the tactics relating to some Amnesty International campaign to liberate a freedom fighter of that name.

'Look Henry,' Peter plunked the table with outspread pudgy fingers, 'it doesn't matter at what point you introduce indeterminacy into the material world, that isn't the issue. The impossibility of free will rests on a misconception of what it is to be truly free; and indeed, the irony of the great superstructure of argument that has been built on top of this category error, is that it – in and of itself – represents the very acting-out of unfreedom – '

' – Bollocks,' Henry countered expertly. 'Total crap. You go round and around Peter, up and down the rhetorical escalator like a child, but really your arguments are naïve, an outgrowth of adolescent cynicism. Your refusal to face up to the freedom of the will is a wish to avoid full moral responsibility – '

'For Christ's sake Henry, give it a bloody rest.'

And so they went on. To begin with Giselle had listened to the argument with close attention. Her eyes flicked over the net of burgundy bottles, from player to player, as they volleyed rubberized sophistries back and forth, struggling to win the point. Eventually she grew weary.

The paradox that it was Beckwood, the polymer scientist working with the testable proofs of science, who clung on to the moral essence of free will, wasn't lost on her. And although she was disappointed by Peter's unwillingness to include her in the debate – apart from an occasional 'Giselle will back this up, she's a philosopher too y'know' – she couldn't help being thrilled once more, as

she had been in his seminars, by the audacity of his pro-
nouncements, the sure rigidity of his mental projections.

Peter kept on creating truth tables to illustrate his more
technical points. At the dinner table these were con-
structed from rolled up pellets of bread, laid out on the
mahogany surface like edible Go counters. From time
to time, Caitlin and June broke off from their intimate
conversation to say things like 'Really Peter, playing
with your food like an infant, is this what you do at High
Table . . .'

Giselle was amazed by how dismissive the women were
of their menfolk. They either ignored them, or joshed them
unmercifully. Their remarks betrayed such condescension,
such refusal to admit any equality with Peter and Henry,
that she was surprised that the men didn't retaliate in any
way. But perhaps they were simply too drunk.

' – That's what Jowett used to say.' They were in the
drawing-room and Henry and Peter were drinking Rémy
Martin out of mismatched tumblers. 'Are you a two-bottle
man, or a three-bottle man!' They guffawed at this.

'Joyce doesn't realize what she's putting up with,' Caitlin
was saying to June. 'If she did, she wouldn't allow them
to bully her in this fashion.' It had transpired that Caitlin
was a landscape gardener as well – and a successful one.
Giselle could figure this out from the famous names that
were inadvertently kicked between them as they discussed ideas, billings, possible commissions, the impossibility of getting good workers.

Giselle had more wine than she should. She was almost
drunk. When she turned her head from the bookcase to
the men's mulberry faces, from these faces to those of the
animated women, her eyes followed on lazily, lurching
against the insides of their sockets as if intoxicated in their
own right.

The voices burred and lowed. Giselle tried to imagine

her hosts as cattle. They fitted the role well, set down on the field of carpet by the pools of wavering light, grazing on conversation.

'You look ready to drop, Giselle.' It was June, her voice maternal, gently concerned.

'I'm, I'm sorry . . .?'

'You better go up to bed my dear, you'll need a good night if you're going to cope with Peter and his hangover in the morning.'

'Oh, yeah, um, s'pose so.' Giselle struggled to her feet.

She said her goodnights. Peter and Henry barely interrupted their conversation, they just waved their glasses at her and made valedictory noises. The women were more polite.

'I do hope you'll be all right in the Rood Room,' said June, 'it can be a bit draughty.'

'Oh I'm sure I will, please don't worry.'

As she tunnelled her way up through the house Giselle felt nothing but relief – relief to have escaped the adults. Even though she was going to bed, she might have been on her way to join the twins, who she could hear chattering and playing records in some mid-distanced room. But what Giselle really wanted was sleep. Sleep and dreams.

In the Rood Room she felt her way gingerly around the shoulder-high screen and across the warped floorboards to the bed. She snapped on the bedside lamp and in that instant the whole space was defined with startling clarity, the Grunters jumbled together in jangling copulation on the screen, its penile coping writhing in the shadows, the plaster reliefs giving a serried leer.

Giselle sat down heavily on the bed and absorbed the charge gathered in the room, the accumulated gasps of time. They bounced off the walls and came into her, nuzzling down in to the warm pit of her lower belly. Giselle was shocked by the feeling – the immediacy of her lust.

The Rood Room seemed to hold her like a lover, cupping her body within its own warm confines.

Giselle had never had any real difficulties with sex. She had moved from riding ponies and horses to riding men and boys easefully, just going up on her sensual stirrups to absorb the shift from a merely physical trot to a psychic canter. But while she could will herself to climax, power herself up on to some kind of free-floating plateau, she knew that the constrictions of her upbringing still remained. Some way inside her, like a twist in a party balloon, they strangled abandon, choked off the flow of desire.

If only someone like Peter Geddes – not Geddes himself of course – but someone like him, someone who plaited the psychic with the physical into a rigid rope, could pull himself into her. Here, in the Rood Room, her orange candle lit and pulsing soft light over the curved ceiling, Giselle could dare to imagine such a possibility – it coming and lancing into her, a naked libertine will, imploding from the noumenal realm into the phenomenal world of her body.

Outside the night insects scratched their legs, as Giselle caressed her own. She ran her palms up from her knees, gathering and then furling back the material of her skirt, conscious of it as a curtain being raised on a living puppet show, her hands – the players – descending from the boards of her belly to the pit of her longing.

Her fingernails snagged at the rubber-band waist of her tights. She peeled them off, together with her pants. The warm coil was dropped by the side of the bed. It was the same with her blouse and her bra. She removed them with the hands of another person. It was those hands that made love to her, the hands that grasped her buttocks and pitched Giselle's body back against the headboard. They whooshed around her breasts, pulling the nipples out to precise points of sensation. They moulded her body with worshipful art, as if it were a wet gobbet of clay being shaped into a votary statue of a fertility goddess.

From the other time of the twins' room, Giselle could faintly hear and dimly recognize the chanting of a current hit: 'Doo-wa yi, yi, yi, dooo-waaa. Yeah-yeah, mm-m-, yeah-yeah.' The painted Grunters flexed their Hanna-Barbera bodies in time to the music, while the foreign fingers – wet now with a gastronome's delight – picked at titbits of Giselle.

When she came it was with a hot flush. So much so, that as she lay on the disordered bed Giselle could almost imagine that she saw steam rising from the juncture of her thighs.

Downstairs Peter Geddes was pissed. The Beckwoods had long gone, and with them had gone the necessity for the propriety of performance that masks unhappiness for the well-bred English family.

June and Peter had reverted to their intimate selves, their rude selves, their hateful and hating selves. The fresh start they'd made that morning, the honest attempt to use happy memories as scaffolding for a brave new marital building, had subsided into the churned-up mud of the present.

June was in the kitchen stacking the dishwasher when Peter's pencilled doodles on the table caught her eye. She went over and peered down at them. This is what she saw:

$p(M)$	$Vm(F)j$	$\rightarrow$	$p(F)j$
T	T		F
F	T		F
T	F		F

She wiped it out with a sweep of her damp J-cloth, and called into the next room, 'You're not free any more Peter!'

'Whassat?' his burning brow poked round the door jamb.

'You're not free any more.'

'Whyssat?' he slurred.

'Because I've obliterated your stupid truth table. You're always saying that the truth about the world is a revealed thing. Well now it's unrevealed. In fact, it's gone altogether.' She was at the sink. Scraping filaments of veal from the dinner plates with horrid knife squeals.

'Oh no, June, you shouldn't have done that, really you shouldn't . . .' Peter was genuinely distressed. He staggered across to the table. In the overhead lighting of the kitchen his drunkenness was even more apparent. 'June, June . . . That was the matrix, the functional cradle that contains us both. Now it's gone . . . Well, I don't know, I just don't know . . .' and in concert with his voice trailing away, his pudgy finger trailed across the damp surface. He raised it to his brimming eyes and contemplated the greyish stain on its pad – all that was left of his freedom.

June slammed the door of the dishwasher. She was, Peter reflected with the hackneyed heaviness of the drunk, even more beautiful when she was angry. 'Right! That's it. I'm not going to listen to this maudlin drivel all night, I'm going to bed. I would suggest you do the same instead of sitting downstairs until five a.m., the way you did when Henry and Caitlin last came over. Honestly, chucking back brandy and listening over and over to the Siegfried Idyll.

'Half of your waking life you seem to think that you're wearing a horned helmet and sitting with the gods in Valhalla, not sporting a greasy mop of thinning hair and drunkenly slumped in your family-fucking-home in Notting-bloody-hamshire.' With that she departed, stamping up the stairs.

For a couple of minutes after she had left the kitchen Peter did nothing. He just swayed back and forth, listening to the gurgling of alcohol in his brain, heavy oil slopping in a rusty sump. Then he summoned himself and dabbing at the light switch with his numb hand managed to kill the lights. He went next door to the sitting-room and with great deliberation turned on the record player, selected an album from the old-fashioned free-standing rack that stood by it, and put it on.

As Wagner's billowing instrumental coloratura filled the room, Peter subsided into an armchair. He spilt a few gills of brandy on to his trousers, but three more managed to hit the tumbler. These he chucked down. The music swelled to fill the space, lowering like a heliotrope grizzly bear. Peter poured himself another brandy, then another and then a fourth.

Some time later he was truly drunk, orbiting his own consciousness in a tiny capsule of awareness that was shooting backwards at speed. He watched, awed, as the dawn of his own sentience sped away from him towards the great slashed crescent of the horizon. Then the toxic confusional darkness came upon him, swallowing him entirely.

The synaptic gimbals had been unslung and Peter's splendidly meticulous gyroscope of ratiocination fell to the jungly floor of his id. He rose and did not know that he did so. He went to the record player and snapped it off – not knowing that he did so. He quit the room. Standing in the misshapen vestibule, the oddly angled point of entry to this disordered household, the philosopher stared into an old mirror – not knowing that he did so.

From out of the mirror there loomed the face of a Grunter. It was dead white, shaped by the utter foreign-ness of the distant past. The Civil War recusant looked at Peter for a while and then slid away into the mirror's bev-elled edge. Peter's head shook itself – hard. His body felt the painful anticipation of the morning and took its mind upstairs.

*

In the Rood Room Giselle lay in a deep swoon. After climaxing she had relapsed thus, and gone to sleep with the twins' pop records still resounding in her ears. But the twins were now asleep as well, and her fine body was still banked up on top of the disordered covers, forming cumulus piles of sweet flesh. A beam of starlight fell across her upper thighs, then extended itself towards the rood screen, where it illuminated the central panel, which depicted five Grunters in a loose bundle of copulation, a fasces of fornication.

Giselle was gorgeous, the fullness of her refulgent in the silvery light. Her auburn pubic hair glowing as if lit from within. Her breath disturbed her breast only just sufficiently to reinforce the impression that she was an artist's model trapped since the Regency in suspended inanimation.

There was a creaking from the corridor, a groaning of larynx and wood. The door squealed on its hinges and Peter Geddes's brandy golem entered the Rood Room.

Giselle awoke at once and sat up. The diamond light from the window was scattered across his brow – outsize spangles. The incubus rubbed at them carelessly. She didn't need to ask who it was, she could see that immediately. She shifted herself back under the covers, adroitly, as if inserting a sliver of ham into a half-eaten sandwich.

'D-Doctor Geddes, is that you?'

'Please,' said the incubus, his voice clear now, unslurred, 'call me Peter.' And then he went on, 'I'm terribly sorry, I must have taken the wrong turning at the top of the stairs. Quite easy to do y'know – even after many lifetimes' residence.'

'Th-that's OK – are you all right?'

'Fine thanks – and you?' He had turned away from her now and was confronting the rood screen. 'Not finding it too hard to sleep in this strange old place?' His voice came to her now as it had done in tutorials, focused, crisply edged by intellect. His outstretched hand traced the line of a Grunter back, in the same way she remembered it tracing the sinuous connectives of his scrawled logical formulae.

As if it were the most natural thing in the world to do, the incubus then moved away from the rood screen and towards where Giselle lay.

'Do you mind if I sit down for a moment?' he said looking down at her.

'No, not at all.' The words pooted from her kissable lips, inappropriate little farts of desire. The incubus sat, inhabiting the warm vacant vee between the ranges of Giselle's calves and thighs. He canted round, his unfocused eyes squeezing their watery gaze into the dilation of her pupils.

'If it wasn't such a trite remark,' the incubus quipped, 'I would tell you how vitally lovely you are at this precise moment – right now.' He bent to kiss her, her urge to resist was as insubstantial as the air that escaped from between their marrying bodies.

His hands unwrapped the covers, her hands unfurled his woolly bunting, until they lay, two tubby people, damp with desire, in the heat of an English summer night.

He kissed her clavicle – the pit of it neatly fitted the trembling ball of his tongue. He tasted the salt of her skin as he ice-cream licked the whole of her upper body, lapping her up. His face went down on her trembling belly and his hands cupped first her round face, then her round shoulders and lastly her rounded breasts. Cupped and kneaded, cupped and kneaded.

To her, the incubus and his touch were more than a release. She couldn't have said why – for she had no reason left now – but he was beautiful. His pendulous belly, his spavined legs, the scurf on his high forehead, the stubble on his jowls, all of it moved her. She grasped the flesh on his back, feeling moles like seeds beneath her palms, she worked at them to cultivate still more of his lust.

The mouth of the incubus was presently in her pubic hair, the tip of his tongue describing ancient arabesques and obscure theurgical symbols on her mons, the deep runnels of her groin, the baby flesh of her inner thighs. The incubus drew in a gout of the urine and mucus smell of her, and savoured it noisily, as if it were the nose of some particularly rambunctious burgundy.

Then his horizontal lips were firmly bracketing her vertical ones, his hands were under her, holding her by the apex of her buttocks, and he ate into her, worried at the very core of her, as if she were some giant watermelon that he must devour to assuage an unquenchable thirst.

Later still the incubus addressed her with the incontrovertible fact of his penis. Entered into her with the logical extension of himself. She was curled up like a copula, a connective, her kneecaps almost in her eye sockets, as he placed himself on top of her. And Giselle went into him, went out of herself, travelled over the curved roof. The incubus was lancing into her from out of that other realm – he was pure, ineffable will, freeing her up with each stroke, dissolving her corporeal self.

His tongue was in her mouth, marauding around the back of her throat. His penis was in her vagina, knocking forcefully at the mouth of her cervix. The shadows of the phalluses on top of the rood screen fell across both their bodies, tiger-striping them in the luminous darkness. The Grunters stared down at the reckless, wrecking bodies with gnostic inappetency.

She came; and the incubus yanked her up in her orgasm, hooking her higher by the pubic bone, until she spun in giddy baroque loops and twirls – pain for pleasure and pleasure for pain. Her cries, her groans, her molar grinds, all were grace notes, useless embroideries on the fact of her abandonment. 'S-s-s-sorry!' It was almost a scream; this remembering, even at the point of no return, the refinements of her upbringing.

They lay in each other's arms for a while, but only a short one. Then the incubus, kissing her to stay silent, departed.

Some while afterwards Giselle heard the sound of a shower pattering in a distant bathroom.

The following morning Giselle went downstairs knowing that this could be the hardest entrance of her life. She had no idea how Peter Geddes was going to play it. His love-making the night before had been so demonic, so intense. It had beached her on the nightmare coast of the dream-land. Would he acknowledge what had passed between them in some way? Would he already have confessed to his wife? Would she find herself back at Grantham station within the hour, her vacation job over and her academic career seriously compromised?

Peter and June were altercating in the kitchen of their ugly house as Giselle appeared at the bottom of the stair-way.

'Honestly Peter!' The gardener was even more beauti-ful this morning, her long blond hair loose in a sheaf around her shoulders. 'You should be ashamed of your-self getting pissed like that on a weekday. What's Giselle,' she gestured towards the guilty research assistant, 'going to think of this household?'

Peter dropped the upper edge of his *Guardian* and looked straight into those guilty eyes. Looked forthright-ly and yet distantly. Looked at her, Giselle realized with a shock, as if she were a member of some other species. He said – and there was no trace of duplicity or guile in his voice – 'Sleep well Giselle? Hope Richard and I didn't dis-turb you during the night?'

'R-Richard?'

'He means Wagner,' said June, placing a large willow-patterned plate of eggs and bacon on the table. 'He always plays Wagner when he gets pissed – thinks it's romantic or something. Silly old fool.' She rumpled Peter's already rumpled hair with what passed for affection, then went on, 'Here's your breakfast Giselle, better eat it while it's hot.'

'Oh, er . . . sorry, thanks.' Giselle sat down.

Peter rattled his paper to the next page. He was feeling pretty ghastly this morning. 'I really oughtn't,' he mused internally, 'get quite that drunk. I'm not as young as I used to be, not as resilient. Still, lucky the old autopilot's so efficient, can't remember a thing after putting on the Idyll . . .' He glanced up from the paper and felt the eyes of his research assistant on him, full of warm love. 'Silly girl,' thought Peter wryly, 'difficult to imagine why, but she must fancy me or something.' His eyes went to the straining spinnakers of her contented bosoms. 'Still, she is a handsome beast . . . pity that I'm not free – in a way.'

Peter Geddes's truth table

p(M)	Vm(F)j	→	p(F)j
T	T		F
F	T		F
T	F		F

or:

Peter is a man. All men want to fuck June. Therefore Peter wants to fuck June.

T = the truth of a component or concluding proposition.
F = the falsity of a component or concluding proposition.

Anu and Le-lea

RAY SHELL

The little ones lay still at last . . .
Breath cut.
Absent from broken chests.
Leadened spears coupled inside wet-fleshed hearts . . .

It was over.
The slaughter had been happy.
Well played.
The shocked moon illuminated the devastation.
They were leaving now; off to seek fresh-bloodied
enemies, then home.
The offering . . . carried aloft at the head of the caravan.
A lone wind skipped among the bones licking the sweet
blood . . .

Anu reached out and felt the wooden hardness.
Kohl-blackened lashes lifted revealing golden irises.
Anu was naked again.
The young Shera warrior guarding him had taken the
clothes that interrupted his view of Anu's perfect
beauty.

'The princess will be pleased . . .' Asrah thought to himself as he planted the crack of his anus firmly over the
bone in the hump of the camel Imperial.

Asrah, high priest to the Orab, had these sixty-seven summers been the faithful one, the prudent one.

Each season's rain he had searched out and found the pearl to be thrown to the swine devo Jer, Asrah's familiar and light to his Shera people. Asrah had kept his covenant with Jer.

The pearl he'd today sucked out of the bowels of desolation was choice . . . rare.

A worthy consort.

A full and eager cistern.

Young enough to lead . . . hard enough to serve pleasure.

Anu was hungry.

It was getting cold.

He didn't understand the words of the strangers who held him aloft in the wooden-yellow-straw-mattressed cage.

Anu looked through the wooden spokes and saw the river walking past him.

He didn't know this river.

He listened to its song.

'Run young master! Rise up and break the chains . . .' The river sang this warning over and over again as the cage marched up and down mountains, through orange plains, stopping only at palmed water holes.

Here the young Shera warrior guarding him passed blood-red meat on a cool grey rock through the wooden spokes.

Anu looked at the carrion.

Blood was forbidden.

Drinking in the hot wonder circling the eyes of the admiring young Shera warrior, Anu pushed the meat away.

Lifting heavy-metal-red shoulders, the young Shera warrior hoisted himself on to the top of the wood-spiked-cage.

He looked with longing at the long-meat roping from between Anu's prince fed thighs.

Anu reclined unperturbed against the yellow pricked straw; straw softened, wetted by the wine-sweat crawling down Anu's unblemished and firm young shoulders to the small of his caved-kissed back.

Anu smiled up at the famished young Shera warrior who was stealthily trying to untie the rope lock that barriered Anu from his grasp.

The young Shera warrior had to touch the offering.

He needed the blessing for the life of his family.

One touch of the found grail, soon to be holy, would put peace among his kinsmen and upon his head the highest honours of his elders.

Lock undone.

The young Shera warrior sat up to position himself for the assault.

He felt a hot sharpness . . . running fire burned through his back.

He was so surprised to see his heart hurled from his chest like a plump pigeon.

Startled open eyes.

Body dropped as if cut from a string.

His blood dripping on to the beautifully astonished Anu face.

Asrah was disturbed.

The dead boy was his eldest nephew.

Only the sons of the Priest family were worthy of the sacred hunt.

Asrah's nephew, by anointing the offering, would have usurped Asrah's authority and claimed for himself the skinned black eagle's beak and eyes that adorned Asrah's head and proclaimed his holy authority.

The boy had to die . . . his body left on top of the

sacrificial cage as witness to his treacherous intent.

Asrah smiled as he thought of the warm red blood dripping on to the offering's body.

Blood of the holy family.

The offering's aura would now be even more powerful . . . even more worthy of the Princess Royal.

Like the plumed, fragile white lilies clustered sumptuously on the perfumed surface of the steaming magic lake, Le-lea luxuriated on top of her rose-petalled bed, sighing regally as her body was moistened with palm oil then powdered with scented gold dust.

The white diamond walls of her sleeping chamber caught the light thrown off the moonlit lake, pitching it on to Le-lea's glistening dusty body.

The entire sleeping chamber sparkled with eyes of a thousand nights, dazzling Le-lea's handmaidens.

Shesan, Le-lea's mother and Queen, stood proudly . . . tearfully next to her husband's mother, the ancient mystic Hagera.

Through the thousands of days and nights like this one, Hagera and Shesan had whispered and cried to Le-lea the secrets and magic places of her Shera people.

Hagera and Shesan both remembered their own night of the golden dust that signalled to the Shera world their evolution to womanhood.

After tonight's magic circle of blood Le-lea would be free to marry.

The thought of rough man-hands touching her secret-softness for the first time made Le-lea's blood rush to her temples.

She felt giddy.

She sighed and nestled even deeper against the damp red-rose petals.

Magda, wife to Asrah, the wisdom of Shera, entered the

chamber bowing low three times before crawling up to Hagera, whispering something into the toothless crone's leathery darkened ear.

'It is time!' Hagera croaked.

In unison, the bronzed handmaidens, like filings drawn to a magnet, picked up the silken coverlet woven from stolen butterfly cocoons and draped it on to Le-lea whose heart thumped out her anticipation as Shesan tied a black shield around her eyes.

This next part of the ceremony was known as the dark secret.

Shesan and Hagera could not reveal its circle to Le-lea.

She would have to walk alone.

Le-lea trembled in excitement as Shesan and Hagera led her . . . the Princess Royal . . . down lemon-scented-torch-lit corridors to King Solgero's sleeping chamber.

Anu could not remember a time when his stomach had rumbled and jumped with such urgency. His throat and mouth ached for wetness; burning like the flamed-sands that lay around his homeland's oasis hamlet.

Anu had lain inside this metal-walled chamber since his captors delivered him out of the wooden cage three days ago.

There had been naked-olive-skinned water boys to bathe and stroke him.

There had been earthen pots to catch the body-water and faeces that dropped from his darkness as black hard rocks; these had been captured and taken away by the water boys as if they were prize rocks to be studied and analysed.

Anu wasn't sure, but he believed that his captors were the family of the bride that Agres his father had spoken of.

'There will come a day when the young prince will be born aloft to sleep inside the beauty of the vessel of our people's future seed . . .'

Agres, his wise old father and King of his land, had smiled at this prophecy. Four nights ago, Anu had lain upon his emerald bed in the bosom of his father's palace and had awakened in a walking wooden cage.

That is why he was not alarmed.

Not even now.

This must be the prophecy fulfilled.

Anu tried to smile as his stomach complained anew.

It wanted feeding.

Each day the water boys had brought dark, hot, wet-bloodied livers and hearts . . . each day Anu looked into the stone bowl . . . his insides leaping, screaming to his mouth as he turned away from the filth . . . each day the water boys had waited silently then taken the stone-bowled-dead-meat away . . . each day Anu waited hopefully for their return, wishing they'd bring him back dishes of green leaves topped with juicy wet grass and the tree fruits that served as meat for the Vir tribe . . . his people.

Anu was distressed and anxious . . . his resolve was weakening.

He was beginning to think how delicious it would be to tear the wet, juicy flesh in his hungry mouth and drink the liquid blood-water.

Anu prayed the water boys would hurry.

The stone door slid open.

He saw the grey stone bowl first.

Anu smiled weakly.

Le-lea felt extremely hot.

The white-diaphanous-butterflied-woven cloak covered her curvaciousness, sweat poured off her and the black shield stung her eyes.

What Le-lea couldn't see was the roaring fire that formed half circles at the head and tail of the bed where King Solgero sat in front of his daughter.

Shesan and Hagera stood behind King Solgero between the fiery half circles.

Everything silent.

Taps and hand signals communicated the progress of the ritual between the adults.

King Solgero stood.

A tall tree of a man.

Back still straight even though fifty summers had passed since he was cut from Hagera's belly.

Olive-green like the olive trees that grew wild on the hillsides that carpeted his fertile, blessed kingdom.

King Solgero had waited through twelve seasons for this moment . . . the moment his eldest daughter was opened.

Le-lea had to be opened so that nothing stood in the way of the offering . . . the offering that would cement the covenant between the devo Jer and his Shera people.

Hagera tapped two times on King Solgero's shoulder.

It was time.

Shesan, tears of joy sprinting down her cheeks, took her daughter's hand . . . led her to the bed . . . Hagera took the butterfly cloak from her shoulders and gently pushed Le-lea down upon the goose-feathered bed.

Le-lea drank a familiar smell into her nostrils.

Before she could run into the familiar fragrance to embrace and know it, Le-lea screamed.

Not from pain.

The shock of the hot oil being rubbed on to and pressed into her vulva made her scream.

There were fingers all over her mystery place . . . Le-lea couldn't tell how many were entering her and caressing the fleshy piece of herself that peeked out of her secret cave.

Le-lea moaned.

Thicker, longer fingers entered her . . . pushed aside soft flesh until their entry was blocked by more flesh . . . the

fingers pulled out slowly . . . only . . . to return in a second
. . . wetted and more urgent . . . pushing . . . pressing
against the door of flesh. The persistent fingers pushed,
prodded . . . played against the door . . . pushing firmly
but gently.

The door would not yield.

A firm and trusted fleshed guard that protected the royal
treasure.

Something thick.

Hard.

Something metallic . . . very long . . . entered now.

Le-lea couldn't breathe.

She felt as if she were being stuffed alive . . . she wanted
to scream but the breath was being stuffed out of her.

The wet-metal battering ram that pushed against the door
of herself again and again was winning the battle.

Le-lea moaned.

The pleasure was new . . . the feeling deep.

At each push a bit of herself gave way, moving the battering ram closer to the prize . . .

It was broken now.

Le-lea felt the dam break.

The virgin-rushing waters wept copiously on to the
fingers of King Solgero who slowly pulled the metal
battering ram out of his daughter's body.

He smiled.

'She is open!' Hagera croaked, weeping as she pressed
bony fingers into Shesan's trembling hand.

Anu picked at the chunks of flesh trapped between his
virgin teeth.

He felt new.

A fire danced up his toes . . . ran up his legs and full thighs
. . . around his backside . . . up his chest . . . shook his mind
around . . . 360 degrees . . . then flew down his chest . . .

stomach . . . resting to burn large in the thick rope of his manhood.

Anu had never seen it rise so majestically . . . it stood strong . . . thick like a lion.

His stomach, full of the strange meat, was comforted.

Anu rubbed his lion down . . . he grabbed at its thickening neck with his fist.

Suddenly fired.

Anu leapt to his feet . . . snorting . . . bucking like the young rams of his father's flock.

Anu danced.

Twirling . . . kicking . . . snorting . . . snapping his song at the metal-caved walls.

He screamed his joy . . . rocking back and forth on his heels like the drunken beggars in the marketplace.

Anu didn't see the wall part and open . . he didn't see the plumed-fragile-white-lilies clustered sumptuously on the perfumed surface of the steaming magic lake.

Anu's eyes were closed.

In ecstasy.

The water boys . . . nude as always . . . led the enthralled Vir prince down the cracked-shelled path into the peace of the water-womb.

The water boys lifted Anu high in the air then lowered his invaded body under the cleansing fountain seven times . . . up then down . . .

Air.

Water.

Fire in the belly.

Earth in the mind.

Ablutions complete.

Offering purified.

Anu was ready.

Le-lea stood waiting in the throne room.

Her handmaidens adjusted the ivory-white feathered cloak that covered her nakedness. She had been bathed, oiled, scented and gold dusted once more.

Le-lea would give audience to the offering.

They would meet at last.

They would be left alone.

Shesan and Hagera had instructed her carefully.

Invisible fingers tapped metal-music pans sending seductive sounds searching every corner of the perfectly domed rock throne room.

The white diamonds in the stone walls were circled in platinum . . . the platinum circled in gold . . . the gold circled in precious rubies . . . emeralds . . . black onyx.

Three peals of the life bell signalled to Le-lea that it was time she sat down upon the cut glass throne.

Le-lea had never sat upon her father's throne . . . its softness belied its gleaming cold austerity. The purple cushions were stuffed with human hair of children dead before their time or shorn on the eve of their thirteenth summer.

There was a ripple in the silk curtain that hung from the ceiling to the floor seventy-five paces from the throne. The shimmering silk separated the throne from the audience area.

Through the ripple of the curtain walked Anu.

He dazzled. Gold. From head to toe.

Anu and Le-lea stared at each other . . . eyes sucking in each other's beauty.

Anu knew he had found his prophecy . . . he bowed his head briefly then looked up into Le-lea's olive-dream face . . . he saw the black mermaid hair that flocked down Le-lea's back like sheep grazing a mount . . . the green yearning emerald eyes . . . the red-rose-petalled lips . . . the ivory-green thighs whispering from underneath the white feathered cloak.

Anu was a gold vision to Le-lea.

Every inch of him was covered in gold satin . . . satin that stretched across his mighty body like the taut sails of a strong-oaked ship . . . satin that cupped the roped-bowl of his manhood . . . emphasizing its size . . . singing promises of its strength.

Le-lea tried to contain herself.

Anu boldly walked forward to the throne. Before he could get much closer, a black marbled divan floated down from the ceiling of the jewelled chamber, temporarily blocking his passage.

At the divan's settling, Le-lea arose from the throne, walked to the top of the divan and signalled Anu to come closer . . . once close she laid him down.

The invisible metal-music pans sang mournfully beyond the black-flowing silk curtains that grew down in layers like a shimmering forest.

Anu lay upon the sweating-black-doe-skinned divan. He closed his eyes . . . felt the blood rush from his stomach down to his gathered rope that rustled like a fighting crowd in the golden trousers.

Le-lea carefully guided the silver dagger underneath Anu's tight golden vest. Le-lea pulled the dagger upward freeing Anu's mountainous shoulders whose muscles jumped forward to greet her like wild mares.

Anu laughed at the cool on his chest . . . longing to ease the fire raging in his loins . . . his closed eyes made him brave.

Anu ripped at the gold cloth that imprisoned his legs and thighs.

Anu won.

He flung away the satin cloth then rubbed against the fired-lion that stood rigidly regal in Le-lea's gasping face. Shesan, her mother and Queen, had blushingly revealed to Le-lea the mystery of the fleshed-battering-ram . . .

Anu's fleshed-battering-ram defied and confounded the prophecy of Shesan and Hagera.

This fleshed-fire-mountain-lion-battering-ram defiantly rising still in her face was more majestic and bewildering than anything the two elder women had ever described.

Le-lea felt a wetness watering inside her . . . her fingers trembled . . . dying to trace the veins popping brown in the fleshed-battering-ram . . . her tongue itched . . . licking Le-lea's lips shyly but wantonly.

Anu opened his golden eyes . . . he saw tiers of olive-sentried-elders with beards hanging down bony shoulders . . . he saw wizened crones . . . eyes-bright . . . staring down upon them . . . he saw mist flying over and under the black silken trees . . . Anu wanted to move but he felt pinned down.

Le-lea looked away from Anu's fleshed-battering-ram and into the perfect innocence of Anu's confused face.

It was time.

Music jumped earnestly from the metal-music pans . . . there was singing . . . rich-earth-voices of a single thunder . . . rain voices . . . tongues of blood and witness . . . there were sighs and wonder in the singing of the old song.

It was a new song to Le-lea.

She had never heard it before.

Anu's eyes were open but sight had fled . . . his limbs lay dead . . . only his manhood-mountain-lion-fire burned lively . . . ready to drip pure life.

Sweat swam down his body.

Anu was cooking.

The long song, sung quietly, carried Le-lea stomach down on to the white rams-wool carpet with the red hole that pointed the way to her secret garden, Anu's only physical contact point with Le-lea's princess body.

Anu's water boys carried Le-lea aloft like the butterflied princess she was.

A lone high-pitched wail echoed down creamily against Anu's dreamed ears . . . he heard as if far off . . . he heard as if on a deeply lost journey . . . he heard as an owl hears . . . softly . . . darkly . . .

Le-lea floated above the heaven of her earthed Anu.

The water boys passed her over him . . . searching for the exact spot for the Le-lea bird to light upon.

The life bell pealed three times.

The spot held . . . it was precise.

The peak of Anu's mountain found the opening of the Le-lea cave.

Down the water boys lowered the Le-lea bird-butterfly . . . down and down.

Anu's moan caresses Le-lea's sigh . . . crying together before twin winging to the top tier to settle on the ears of King Solgero and his teared Queen Shesan . . . Hagera rocks silently in her balcony above the head of Le-lea where she can see everything . . . down and up . . . down and up . . . slowly . . . tightly . . . teasingly . . . mountain into cave . . . mouth swallowing meat . . . only touching genitally . . . Le-lea fears she won't be able to contain herself . . . she wills herself to lay there, letting the water boys lower and raise her violent expectations which have been more than filled . . . overflowing fulfilment . . . Le-lea struggles against tearing through her elevator canopy . . . wishing to spring herself on to Anu's mountain to scale the entire landscape of his body unencumbered . . . she had never tasted his salty lips . . . had never felt his burnished hands anywhere . . . had never held even one finger . . . and yet his mountain engulfs her . . . she knows love.

This strange offering kindles her . . . boils her body . . . bubbles her as the black oil bubbles in the deep rock next to Anu's divan.

Anu walks in a cloud . . . beyond the rainbow where his

mind now rests . . . his King father and Queen mother call to him . . . beckoning him forward . . . his mother cries pearl tears of welcome . . . his father clasps Anu to his bosom . . . 'You've done well . . . our future secured . . .' . . . Anu smiles and remembers Le-lea.

Le-lea, wet everywhere, gasps, her breath leaving her in rocket bursts.

More water boys join the original four . . . the flying becomes as an eagle's.

Fast.

Sharp.

Down.Up.Down.Up.Faster with the drum . . . faster than the song . . . Anu's fire rages even fiercer . . . his volcano near to boiling point . . . Le-lea on the verge of faintness . . . the drums beating faster . . . updownupdown . . . each down beat thumped and screamed . . . back and forth . . . up and down the tiers of the holy rock. Anu's lava rising . . . rising, now shooting, now hitting the prize spot. Le-lea holding her breath . . . and then it hits . . . her throat screams the note the world, her life, has waited these thirteen summers to hear.

Before the scream can die . . . even before Anu's volcano-lava rush finishes its spurt, his mountain is hewn down . . . his fleshed-battering-ram is scythed off at the root and flung into the boiling black oil erect . . . immortalized in metal forever . . . ready for the next opening of a Shera Royal Princess.

Blood streams upwards from the gaping crater between the Prince Anu thighs . . . he never notices . . . he is far away kissing sky maidens in a purple cloud . . . the spurting blood misses Princess Le-lea who already has flown away out of view.

Star Light; Star Bright

A Euro Story

B A R B A R A   T R A P I D O

Peter had not always been Peter. Until the day that his mother had met the English schoolmaster on the beach in Lyme Regis, he had known himself to be Pietro, though his grandmother had always called him Pierre.

Until he was five, he had lived alone with his mother at the top of a tall grey apartment house in Paris, five minutes from the Luxembourg Gardens. He had tried hard not to remember it, not because he had disliked his time there, but because for quite a while now he had striven assiduously to be English. In the language class at school, he spoke French competently but not so well that his peers would revert to calling him 'grenouille' or 'Mon-sewer Jérémie Pêche-à-ligne'.

He remembered that he had slept in a sort of walk-in cupboard off his mother's attic bedroom – a triangular prism like a Toblerone box, so small that his mattress had covered all the floor space. At the weekends he had spread his toys over the floor of his mother's bedroom on a carpet that was pale grey. He remembered that his five cloth animals had lived on the sill of his mother's bedroom window, beyond which was a maze of grey slate roofs with leaded seams. Pigeons had strutted over the roof ridges and sometimes he had seen them stalked by a sure-footed, piebald cat.

He knew that his father, who was dead, had been a

racing driver, but – as a person who related more to the sky than the ground – it had been a small step for his imagination to reconstruct the man as an air pilot who would one night fly over the rooftops in a biplane and perch, like the pigeons, on one of the roof ridges. Peter trembled to think of his father proceeding inexorably toward the window in his great goggles and climbing in like Peter Pan.

He was afraid of Peter Pan. He was afraid that his father would come back. He was afraid that *le père Noël* would come down the chimney. He was afraid of almost everything except his own loneliness. He considered that the stars made satisfactory friends. Being an only child, an indoor child, a rooftop child, he interacted well with the stars. He knew that the nearest galaxy to our own was sixteen million light years away and that this could be written as 16×10^5. He knew that the Arabs had invented the astrolabe. He knew that the stars were great luminous balls of gasses and that young stars evolved, over millions of years, into Red Giants and White Dwarfs. He knew the Twins and the Ram and the Great Bear and the Little Bear. He knew the story of Ariadne's Crown. He knew that Venus was the morning and the evening star. He knew Syrius the Dog Star. He knew that their isolation from each other was so great that it could be measured only in unimaginable waves of movement. He knew that their isolation was benign.

On the April day that had changed everything, Peter was on the beach in Lyme Regis, playing tennis with his mother. He had accompanied her there on a photographic assignment because his grandmother could not have him. She had recently acquired a hip replacement and was only two weeks out of hospital. They had travelled from Paris in an aeroplane reassuringly unlike the one that his father would land on the rooftops and had stayed in a hotel near the sea. Peter could remember how he had seen the plastic tennis set in a newsagent's window and had whined for it. Two yellow racquets and four cheap yellow balls made of sponge foam.

He was not an athletic child, but he had seen Björn Borg on his grandmother's television set and the bright yellow colour of the racquets and the balls had attracted him.

He could remember his disappointment and frustration at finding out how difficult the game was. When Maman served, the rubbishy, fake balls always blew on the wind and landed wide, which meant that he consumed his time in retrieving them. It was unpleasant to walk on the beach. It was like walking in lead boots and, whenever he himself tried to serve, the balls, after twirling in the air over his head, would evade the inept swipe of his racquet and fall immediately behind him.

As the hour got closer to lunch, Peter became intransigent and irritable. He whined that it was all not fair and that it was all Maman's fault. And Maman was wearing that familiar, half-concentrating look which meant that, while her body was with him, her mind was far away. Neither she nor his grandmother had ever been any good at playing.

Peter threw the ball up harder than ever and – having swiped the air once more, this time with angry vigour – he flung the racquet after it. It flew in an anti-clockwise arc and landed somewhere behind him.

'Pietro!' Maman said, and then she said, 'Oh excuse me, sir,' and she sounded rather embarrassed. 'Pietro,' she said. '*Va chercher la raquette et demande pardon au monsieur.*'

Peter turned to see that, some distance behind him and seated on a deckchair, was an elderly man dressed in the collar of a *curé* and wearing an old straw hat. He was sitting alongside a younger man who had looked up from reading a newspaper. He saw that the old man had the plastic racquet in his hand.

'*Non!*' Peter said, his shyness sounding like bad manners. '*Non!*' But, to his horror, the old man then rose from his chair and walked purposefully toward him. Peter froze to the spot. It took him some moments to realize that the assailed person was advancing in a spirit of cordiality.

'My word, young man,' the old man said. 'This is really no way to play tennis.'

Gentille had been both charmed and diverted by the old man. So few people in this life conformed to type, she reflected, and here was a small, absurd slice of storybook England; an old cleric in a straw hat and rolled trousers who came forward on a beach to work at a small child's serve. To watch him with her son caused her a small glow of pleasure which enlivened her pale, impassive face. There was a quietness about Gentille, a complete absence of fuss and flap, which men often found appealing. Because of it they mistakenly assumed her to be vulnerable, but Gentille was completely sure of herself.

Meanwhile the old man had positioned the racquet in Peter's hand and, having gestured to indicate an invisible tennis net, had taken hold of the boy's right arm and shoulder. Gentille knew that Peter understood not a word of what the old man said, but he was responding readily to the spirit of the instruction.

'Now then,' the old man was saying. 'Right shoulder away from the net. Good boy! That's the ticket! That is quite definitely one hundred per cent better!'

Gentille had not only taken to the old man. She had arrived with a predisposition toward certain things English. This was her way of being just slightly anti-French. While she seemed to people in England the very epitome of all things French, Gentille was an outsider by history and inclination. She came from a family of outsiders.

Her maternal grandmother had been a fair-skinned, blue-eyed Polish Jew who, being in the final stages of labour when the Gestapo had raided the hospital, had miraculously survived the fatal evacuation by crawling, mid-spasm, into a dark recess for fear of being trampled underfoot. An hour later she had given birth, all alone, in an unlit linen store, had wrapped her daughter in a towel and had licked the mucus from the baby's eyes. She knew that everything about her former life was over. Young, recently married and very much in love, she knew that she no longer had a home or a family and that she would never again see her husband. Over the next few years, in a macabre and protracted odyssey to which she had never properly given voice, she had effectively walked to France. There she was taken in by an ailing, middle-aged storekeeper and put to work in the shop.

At some time thereafter she married the storekeeper. The arrangement was convenient to both. She was young and strong and the storekeeper needed her labour. He was possessed of an income and an identity which she and her small daughter lacked.

The daughter was Peter's grandmother. By the time she was eight years old, the storekeeper was a bed-ridden old man with ravaged lungs and rheumy eyes, a skeletal figure in an upstairs room. Then he was dead. She had nothing belonging to her real father; no photograph, no watch, no small book of verse awarded in school for good attendance, and her mother – who had learned the wisdom of speaking as little as possible – had never been expansive in bequeathing to her the past. What she did bequeath was that quietude and muted emotional response which had been borne out of her own ruptured life experience,

and Peter's grandmother had bequeathed it, in turn, to
Gentille.

Since Gentille's own father, aged twenty-six, had died
within two hours in a freak attack of undiagnosed viral
pneumonia, she too had come to maturity in the absence
of a male parent. It seemed the natural state of things. She
had grown up a bright, poised and diligent girl with a
quiet, private manner and a fine pale face. Having done
very well at school, she had gone, young, to university in
Paris, from which she had taken a step sideways into
photo-journalism.

   Soon afterwards, while on an assignment in Turin, she
had attracted the eye of one Aldo Rusconi, a racing driver.
The marriage had been hasty, unsuitable and brief.
Gentille's austerity had been ill-matched with her husband's dare-devil hedonism and she had taken a prompt,
uncompromising stand against his ongoing sexual
promiscuity. Within fourteen months she had returned to
Paris with a very young baby and had taken a job, first in
the picture department of a newspaper and then on a
magazine. At the same time she had persuaded her mother to take an apartment nearby and to assume the daycare
of the child.

   By the time Peter was four years old, his mother was
twenty-seven and his father, like all the fathers in his family, was dead. Gentille's first awareness of her estranged
husband's death came when she saw the pictures of his
burning vehicle in the offices of her workplace. She had
subsequently inherited some money and, having no need
of it herself, she had put it aside for Peter. She was a com-
petent, hard-working professional woman and she
earned a decent salary. Aldo's death in itself had had
almost no effect on her. She already knew that nothing in
this life was permanent; that change came, for good or ill,

and that, when it came, one moved on. Aldo belonged to the past and the past, by its very nature, was not there.

Now it was midday and she wanted to get on. 'You are very kind, sir,' she said. 'But Pietro keeps you from your lunch.'

The old man, preoccupied, merely gestured vaguely toward the deckchairs. 'Take a seat, dear lady,' he said. 'My son will take care of you, I'm sure.'

Gentille was not accustomed to being patronized with male courtesies and was about to stand her ground when her eyes met those of the younger man. She saw that these were dark brown and sparkling and that they spoke ironic amusement against the old man's put-down. Her facial expression responded to this in kind. The young man removed his newspaper from the vacant chair beside him and rose politely as she approached.

'You mustn't let my father bully you,' he said. He was unaware that Gentille let nobody bully her.

'Your father is very kind,' she said.

'Yes,' said the younger man. 'Yes he is.'

She offered him her hand. 'I am Gentille Rusconi,' she said.

'I'm Roland Dent,' he said.

It was clear from the vantage point of the deckchairs that Peter was having the time of his life. So was his companion. The old man had been feeling the lack of grandchildren. One of his daughters, who was in broadcasting, lived, childlessly, with a businessman in Dulwich, while the other, who was married with two small daughters, lived somewhat inaccessibly in Vancouver. As for dear Roland, he was thirty-one and unattached. Puzzling, that, the old man thought. His son was a thoroughly decent young man, capable, considerate and easy on the eye. Yet he had had, after a series of trifling, youthful alliances, only one serious passion, some five years earlier, for a shy young student at Oxford. The affair had ended badly and the poor boy had been most terribly cut up. Still, five years was five years after all and the boy was distinctly eligible.

In the minutes that followed, Roland learned that Gentille was a photo-journalist on a French magazine and Gentille learned that Roland was a schoolmaster who taught mathematics in a boys' boarding school in Worcestershire. She learned that he was spending some days with his parents who had recently retired to a woodland cottage in the Dorset countryside some two miles from the sea and that the old man was a retired army chaplain who occasionally stood in for local clergymen when they were ill or taking a holiday.

Peter learned that the old man's name was also Peter.

'So you're Pietro, eh?' the old man said. 'That's Peter. Like me. I'm Peter too. Peter Dent.' And they shook hands solemnly. 'Ever set a rabbit trap old man?'

Peter went to tea at the cottage next day. He went with his mother. Roland drove out to fetch them from the hotel. The cottage was not visible until one came upon it because it lay, in densely wooded terrain, down a winding half-mile lane and over a small bridge that crossed a stream. The stream formed the boundary of the garden at the front and behind was a ring of old oak trees. Beyond these, and rising steeply, lay acres of mixed woodland. The old man, when he came out to greet them, had a jaunty little dog at his heels with a pirate patch over one eye who wagged his tail and wiggled his back ecstatically.

'Hello there,' said the old man. 'Syrius, meet Pietro.' Peter was already crouching to receive the canine kisses.

'*Alors, comme l'étoile?*' he said, excitedly.

'Good man,' the old man said. 'Well done, Peter! Yes indeed. *Etoile*, just so. You have made the acquaintance of Syrius the Dog Star. The Star Dog, as he prefers to think of himself. I'm afraid that most people mistakenly believe his name to be "Serious". He's had to put up with the indignity.'

Inside the house, which they entered through the kitchen door, Peter and his mother met the old man's wife who was tall and grey-haired and beautiful. The kitchen had a wood-burning stove and flowery china displayed on shelves. The table was laid with a cloth and on it sat a fruit cake and a plate of scones along with little pots of jam and cream. The teapot wore a sleeveless silver jacket, hinged in the middle, over the orb of its fat body, but with its spout and its handle sticking out.

In the living-room there was a fireplace with what looked like a small iron cupboard on legs. It had red glass windows through which you could see the glow of burning wood and, beside it, on the hearth stone, judiciously placed, lay a pile of big, hard-covered books with pictures of moles and armadillos and aeroplanes and soldiers in uniform. Inside they all said 'Peter Dent' in a childish, pre-war hand.

Beyond the cottage, down a crunching gravel path, lay a well-house, like a glorified shed, full of choppers and storm lanterns and pulleys and planks of wood. After tea, the old man took Peter, along with Serious Syrius the Star Dog, into a field to check rabbit traps. Peter was beside himself with joy and returned to the cottage armed with several straight sticks which he sharpened into spears. He did so with the active assistance of the old man who had proffered a bone-handled Bowie knife.

'*Fais attention*, Pietro!' Gentille said.

'Dear,' the old woman said solicitously. 'I really do not think that the boy has had much experience with knives.'

'Don't fuss, Heather,' the old man said. 'It's a funny thing,' he said to Peter. 'Charming creatures, women, but they're always inclined to fuss.'

While Gentille talked to the old man's wife, Roland excused himself, saying that he had letters to post and would walk the mile into the village to do so. He longed for air and exercise since, damn it, the oldies couldn't be sweeter, but they would insist on a fire, even on a warm April evening. Furthermore, he felt the party to be perfectly balanced without him. His mother had taken to the French woman and his father to the French woman's boy. He spent all his working life with boys and right then he was on holiday. Plus it had to be admitted that the French woman's boy was more than a little bit wet, poor kiddo, doubtless through no fault of his own.

Yet on his return, Gentille had expressed such unequivocal enthusiasm for the local drama society's production of *The Provoked Husband* that he had found himself, graciously on cue, suggesting they attend it together and leave Pietro to spend the night with his parents.

The French woman had surprised him by turning out to be thoroughly clued up on Restoration comedy – far more so than he – and he found her an agreeable companion, thoughtful, calm and unaffected.

And, next morning, after returning from an hour's ride, he had humoured his father by agreeing to trot tamely down a section of the lane and back, with the boy sitting before him on the saddle. Roland could feel the boy's terror against his own body but, once safely back on the ground, the child had turned it all into hostility.

'*Mon père n'aime pas les chevaux,*' he said. '*Il préfère aller par avion.*'

*

It was Gentille who made the first move. She had been thinking about Roland intermittently during certain evenings alone after work. A series of pleasurable images had lingered after her return to Paris; an image of Roland drinking beer with her in the churchyard during the interval of that ridiculous English play – all dolts and parsons and lechery; an image of Roland waxing his size 48 walking boots on the doorstep of his parents' charming kitchen. Then there had been all those photographs that had stood in frames on the piano – photographs of Roland almost invariably engaged in field sports, water sports and cook-outs. His evident sportiness entertained her with its novelty, since her own life was – had always been – conspicuously unathletic.

Roland was marking sixth form maths books when the telephone rang. He picked it up immediately, sounding a little preoccupied.

'Gentille,' he said cordially, though he had not been thinking about her at all.

'You are well?' she said.

'Most certainly,' said Roland, who was never ill. 'Thank you. And you?'

'Oh yes,' she said, dismissively, wishing to proceed to other business. 'And you are busy? But you will have a short holiday next week.'

Roland's laugh was like an admission. 'You're very well informed,' he said.

'Of course,' Gentille said. 'I am a journalist.' Roland said nothing. He waited for her to go on. 'I invite you to spend your holiday with me in Paris,' she said.

He was startled and disarmed by her directness. 'Well – ' he said.

'You know Paris, of course?' she said.

It came to him, suddenly, that he had never properly been there. Once, changing trains on his way to a climbing fortnight in the Alps. Once again, as a schoolboy, on a day trip during a memorably dreadful French 'exchange', throughout which the host family had alternated between ignoring him and watching him with interest as he struggled to consume jellied tripe – 'la treep', as he still thought of it with a shudder. He had subsequently gone on to acquire a perfectly decent pass in O level French, but he still, in his heart, associated the language not only with animal innards, but with the frightful Madame Lazarre, who had swept into his prep school classroom once a week to fire incomprehensible questions. For many years, he had considered that her '*Réponds en français!*' sounded suspiciously like 'Rapunzel!'

'No,' Roland said. 'No, hardly at all. I spent a little time just north of Paris once. It's going back a bit.'

'So you will come?' she said. Roland hesitated. 'Pietro goes to my mother,' she said. 'The time will be quite free.' After a pause, she said, 'I have the Musée d'Orsay here, just down the street . . . There are of course many little restaurants and bars . . .' Then she said, 'Or perhaps a trip to the country . . .'

Quite suddenly, Roland thought why not? Why not go? Open the mind. Breathe new air. A long weekend in a handsome foreign city not an hour away by plane – and in the company of a perfectly acceptable woman. After all, where's your spirit? He felt shamed by his habitual insularity which drove him to spend his half-term holidays walking the Pennines, or canoeing from Ross-on-Wye to Tintern. Once, admittedly, he had gone to see his sister in Vancouver.

'How very kind of you to ask me,' he said.

And so it was arranged between them.

Roland had the taxi drop him off at the corner near the man who sold oysters from a wooden counter in the street. He collected the key from the art dealer with the Dufy seascape in the window and he climbed the fifty-eight stairs to the apartment. Gentille's front door was painted pale matt grey. It opened on to a large, under-furnished room, the bare floorboards and walls of which had been painted pale matt grey. She had left coffee for him in a pale grey thermal jug and alongside the jug stood an outsize, pale grey cup and saucer, the cup shallow and bowl-shaped. A couple of brioches were evident, wrapped in a pale grey napkin. They sat – jug, cup and brioches – like a monochrome still life, upon a matt grey trestle table which was otherwise bare, except that Gentille had wedged a sheet of pale grey Ingres paper under the saucer. On it she had written *'Bon appétit!'*

The room possessed two tall, uncurtained windows fitted with grey-painted shutters, now fixed open. The windows overlooked similarly tall, grey apartment houses across the narrow street. Under the windows were two solid, pale grey armchairs of curving art deco design, separated by a pale, matt grey coffee table upon which stood a vase, stippled in tones of grey and containing a dozen matt grey tulips carved out of wood.

Otherwise, the room contained a single shelf of books, a small CD player and a chrome replica, the size of a shoe-box, of a 1950s Citroën DS. This last startled him, being the very model of a car he had once possessed and cherished before his girlfriend – fiancée as he had then thought of her – had driven it into the Tees on what had turned out to be quite the most miserable day of his life.

He turned quickly from the model and looked around. The room was the only one on that level, except for a tiny kitchen that was wedged under a flight of turret-like, winding stairs. In the kitchen, Roland registered that Gentille possessed a small, table-top fridge and a glazed sink in which there lay two pale matt grey dinner plates and two wine glasses, unwashed but neatly stacked. He wondered idly who had dined with her the previous night, or had it been the boy? Various utensils and two small pans hung from a grey-painted, perforated board fixed to the wall above a small cooker on cabriole legs. A packet of Gitanes lay open on the workboard alongside a giant grey ashtray.

Roland returned to the living-room and poured himself some coffee. Gentille had made it fiercely strong and the establishment revealed no sign of sugar or milk. He gulped it, wincing, and then sat down on one of the arm-chairs to eat the brioches. As he adjusted to the spare, immaculate space, he began to imagine that Gentille was sitting in the other armchair, her long legs stretched out before her, her ankles crossed, her feet in those curious, medieval, velvety shoes that came up over her insteps. He felt the scrutiny of her shadowy grey eyes and began to feel out of place. Why the hell was it all so grey? He was not, in the main, a defiant person, but now he felt that all the colours about his person – his clothes, his hair, his skin, his travelling bag – were as attributes constituted in defiance of an inviolable orthodoxy.

Gentille appeared in the lunch hour and walked with him to a café where they ate a few small clams and a salad made with dandelion leaves. After that she smoked her Gitanes and smiled and said very little and drank black coffee. Roland drank beer and felt hungry and said less. Then they walked through the Luxembourg Gardens until they got to the Avenue de l'Observatoire, where Gentille explained that, since her office was within a stone's throw, he should return.

' – Before you become lost,' she said.

'I don't "become lost",' Roland said, feeling an irrita-tion which he had not yet diagnosed as proceeding from the inadequacy of his lunch. 'I am quite capable of taking bearings.'

'Ah,' Gentille said. 'Then you may walk with me a little further.'

That night she took him to a Japanese restaurant in the Rue Grégoire du Tour, where she taunted his stomach with dainty portions of bean curd jelly and little parcels of raw fish. After that he slept on an air bed on the floor of her living-room.

On Saturday morning, Gentille went in to work, but she returned at midday and walked out with him along the Quai de la Tournelle and on to the Ile St Louis, through a street of small, exclusive clothing boutiques. One of these she suddenly, spontaneously entered and, once inside, obliged him to sit on a frail, bentwood chair, while both she and the sales assistant solicited his opinion of a pale, sack-like garment with far too many buttons in which Gentille emerged from the changing room.

From the boutique they made their way, sans lunch and via two elderly churches rather too heavy with the trappings of idolatry, and two small bars, where Roland drank Belgian beer and Gentille drank club soda with a dash of what looked like liquid raspberry jam, to the Musée d'Orsay, where she stood, silent and reverent, for fully twelve minutes, before a small, severe wooden work table designed by Philip Webb of Oxford in 1931.

She made supper for him in the apartment; a casual affair as it seemed to him, following upon several tots of Macallan's and consisting of two very small poached eggs smelling faintly of fish and served on fine-cut circles of fried bread the size of cross-sections through tennis balls. Intermittently, she filled their glasses with white wine. He was uncomfortably aware, throughout the meal, of an insistently mournful female voice emanating from the CD player.

Roland ate as slowly as he could and leaned back to

watch Gentille smoke. As the hour for sleep became inevitable, Gentille, after a brief spell in the bathroom while he cleared away the plates, enquired, with that slightly taunting smile which had begun to get on his nerves: 'And you will be happy again to sleep here on the floor?'

'Perfectly happy, thank you,' Roland said and then he lay awake, listening to the sound of her feet on the floor above as she crossed and re-crossed the room. He wondered what on earth it was like up there, since he had not ventured beyond her bathroom – a place which had struck him as being quite excessively cluttered with cosmetic jars and unguents for a woman who appeared to wear no make-up.

On Sunday morning Gentille appeared barefoot from the turret and wearing a grey silk kimono. Roland woke to the aroma of her bath oil which had infused the apartment, cloyingly borne on steam. She brought two cups of coffee on a tray and four very small soldiers of toast with a measure of pink grapefruit marmalade. When she had placed the tray on the floor, she sat down beside it alongside the air bed.

'*Voici ton petit déjeuner,*' she said. '*Tu as bien dormi?*' He sat up, shirtless, to lean his head uncomfortably against the wall and took note that the coffee, to his relief, had been made with milk. He considered the possibility that she was addressing him in French in order to put him at a disadvantage. Rapunzel. Rapunzel. *Réponds en français!*

How cold she is, how snide, he thought, and his heart went out to the absent Pietro, whose stamp was nowhere to be seen in the apartment. Not that he was one to beatify the kiddiwinks – and, God only knew, he had had his fair share of dealings with the addle-brained, 'child-centred' parent – but where was there any evidence of the boy? Where were his toys, his drawings, his plastic soldiers? Where were all those bog-roll and cornflake-box constructions that his sister's kids bore home from playgroup? Where was the child's Peter Rabbit mug, so to speak? Or was the poor infant required to quaff his Ribena from one of those punitive matt grey coffee cups?

'*Enfin*,' she said. '*Veux-tu aller à Versailles aujourd'hui? On pourrait faire un tour de bicyclette.*'

'Just out of interest,' he said. 'Why are you speaking to me in French?'

Gentille uttered a small, rippling laugh. '*Parce que nous sommes en France!*' she said.

She kept a grey 2CV in the garden of a friend's house in the suburbs. They went to fetch it on the Métro. Then they drove to Versailles. Once there, they rented bicycles and cycled through the park. It was most invigorating, Roland thought, to have the wind in one's face, and the landscaping was exquisite. And then there was that absurd little Toytown milking shed where the queen had played dairymaid while her subjects groaned under their taxes and starved. Roland's stomach cried out in sympathy. He wondered, as they drove back in almost total silence, how it was that Gentille appeared to have no need to punctuate the hours with provender, or did she distill her nectar from the air?

Suddenly Gentille, without any visible reason, brought the car to a pointed halt along a quiet stretch of road. She sat for a while with her hands in her lap and said nothing.

'So,' she said eventually. 'Now you have seen Paris.'

'Yes,' he said.

'And you have seen Versailles,' she said.

'Yes,' Roland said.

'And you have seen the inside of my apartment and the inside of my car,' she said.

'Gentille – ' Roland said.

She made a small, elegant, unfathomable gesture with her hands.

'Gentille – ' he said again and he stopped. He thought, ought I to kiss her? But he merely sighed and did nothing. 'Gentille, I'm sorry,' he said and they sat silent for a while longer.

'There is another woman,' she said eventually.

'No,' Roland said. 'As a matter of fact, no, there isn't.'

She turned her eyes on him, examining his face. 'But there was,' she said astutely.

'Oh gosh,' Roland said. 'But so long ago. Really. Hardly even a woman. A girl, I suppose. What I mean is, the women I've met ever since – well – I haven't been able to persuade myself that any of them mattered, if you know what I mean.'

'And I?' Gentille said.

'I don't know,' Roland said. 'Forgive me, Gentille, but I can't say.'

After a long pause, she said, 'And the girl?'

'I believed that she cared for me,' Roland said, reluctantly. 'I believed that she really cared for me, you see. She was very shy. Very undemonstrative – but she had given me to understand – ' he stopped. 'I was wrong,' he said curtly. 'I'd misread her.' Then he was silent for so long that she thought he had given up his narrative. 'I propositioned her,' he said bluntly. 'I put my arm around her as she was driving my car over a bridge. I – well we *had* been going out together for almost a year,' he said. 'She was so determined to avoid me that she drove my car into the river.'

'You *forced* her?' Gentille said, in disbelief.

'Good Lord no,' Roland said. 'I merely said, rather categorically, that I felt the time had come.'

'And for this she drive your car into the river?' Gentille said.

'Drove,' Roland said, correcting her involuntarily. 'Yes.' He was beginning to wish that he had never embarked on the disclosure.

'And you were *in* the car?' she said. 'Both of you?'

'Yes,' Roland said. 'I shattered a window. I got us out. She'd had a bad blow to the head.' Gentille looked him over. Then she took up his right arm which was bare from the elbow and turned it over and stared at it closely, as if searching it for scars.

'This girl,' she said. 'You saved her life.'

'Well,' Roland said, wishing to deflect tribute. 'Yes. End of car, unfortunately. Beautiful old Citroën. Just like the one in your living-room, actually. How do you come to have it?'

Gentille ignored the question. 'And now,' she said, pointedly, never taking her eyes off his face. 'Because of this . . . this ridiculous . . . this hysterical English virgin, you sleep in my apartment two nights on the floor and you are with me like a monk.'

'Good Lord – ' Roland said. 'Gentille – '

'Though I feed you with *palourdes* and *salade angevine* in the Rue Jacob and I take you in the Musée d'Orsay to make homage to Mr Webb, your own countryman – '

'Gentille – ' Roland said.

' – and I cook for you myself two beautiful eggs in the stock from mussels, and I play for you while you eat, Gluck's most exquisite *"J'ai perdu mon Eurydice"*. I wake you in my silk robe from the Kenzo house –'

'Gentille – ' Roland said.

'I give you only my most precious Arabian coffee, ground with cardamom pods, and still you cannot climb the few small steps to where I sleep – '

'Good God,' Roland said and he winced. 'Gentille. What an idiot I've been. Hundred per cent brainless philistine. Dear girl, can you forgive me?'

In reply, Gentille leaned forward and kissed him on the mouth. As he gave himself up to the experience, he forgot completely that he was hungry. He was only aware of his thirst. The thirst was like that of a pilgrim in a desert place who has finally come upon a well. Then she drove him back in silence. In silence they parked the car and took the Métro into the centre. In silence they climbed the turret stairs beyond the bathroom to where Gentille's bed lay under the exposed roofbeam, like a tranquil grey island in the middle of the floor. To touch her was like putting on silk. Her cold, well-pumiced heels made shock waves judder through his abdomen. Roland had never before felt anything quite so extraordinary.

When he awoke it was the next morning. He saw that the light came in through a small dormer window that gave on to grey slate roofs and that five cloth animals sat in a line on the sill. He saw that the boy's Lego bricks were stacked in the corner in a wooden box with rope handles. Then he saw that Gentille was standing in the doorway holding that ominously small tray.

'*Bonjour*,' she said. '*Tu as bien dormi?*' This time it didn't get on his nerves, but the sight of the tray made him panic as his stomach cried out against its contents.

'Gentille,' he said. 'Tilly. Dear one. Can I tell you something? I'm starving. I've been starving ever since I got here. If you don't want me to expire, don't even think of offering me those little slivers of nursery toast with that pink marmalade. Don't even think of it.'

Gentille blinked. 'You may eat anything you like,' she said. 'If you will tell me what it is you like . . .'

Roland thought that maybe he wanted half a sheep on a platter, dished up with a two gallon bucketful of *pommes frites*. Or perhaps he wanted five *poulets*, roasted together on a spit.

'Tilly,' he said, 'I'll eat anything. Frankly, I'm so bloody hungry I could eat a horse.'

Gentille put down the tray and advanced upon the bed.

'Never,' she said and she began to draw down the sheet.

'Gentille – ' he said. 'Please. Tilly, no. I'm too hungry. I need to pee. I beg you – '

'Horse?' she said. 'But I think an Englishman will never eat a horse.'

When Peter returned, Roland had already taken the Métro for Charles de Gaulle. There was nothing observably different about the apartment, except that the chrome replica of the 1950s Citroën had gone. His mother's bed stood neatly made in the middle of the floor and his animals were waiting for him in a line along the windowsill. Through the window he saw that the piebald cat was once again stalking the pigeons. Everything was the same, except that everything had changed.

His mother faced the change, when it came, with a predictable absence of nostalgia. She moved on. For Peter, it was more difficult. No less so because he had initiated the change himself. He had played tennis on a beach in England. He had fallen in love with an old man and a well-house and a dog named after the Dog Star. He had not anticipated that his mother would fall in love as well.

The stars were still the same and they were very clear, some nights, from the dormitory windows, but it was difficult, in an English boarding school, to achieve that benign isolation. And, in the classroom, his own particular Madame Lazarre was called Madame Maloret.

'I used to live in Paris,' Peter said, reluctantly, when she quizzed him.

'*En français, s'il vous plaît!*' she said.

'*J'ai habité une fois à Paris,*' Peter said, struggling against his own facility.

'*Grenouille,*' said a voice behind him. '*Mon-sewer Jérémie Pêche-à-ligne.*'

Short Eyes and the Green Dice

E L I Z A B E T H   Y O U N G

Today I read a book about Albert Fish, the cannibal. He killed and ate a little girl called Grace Budd. I walked around repeating 'Grace Budd, Grace Budd' to myself. It was the perfect name. She was a bud that never flowered. I went to the mall. More stores had been boarded up. It was getting dark. I watched the kids flying down the ramps on their two-wheeled skates. They looked like fire-flies. It was cold so I went home. Miss MacDonald phoned to reschedule our meeting. She is my probation officer. She told me to keep a journal. I wish someone would write a book about me! Not as an Albert Fish of course! Although perhaps that would be better than nothing.

Slept badly. Got up early and made toast. Watched the postman from behind the curtain. There was nothing for me. It was a very misty morning. The bushes were grey as gravestones. Looked in the mirror for a long time and pounded my gut. 'Dissolve, dissolve' I chanted. Decided to take Miss MacDonald's advice and shave off my beard. Afterwards my skin was red and scrapy. Read a book about Ted Bundy. In some photographs he looks very glamorous and in others quite ordinary. Wish I was taller. And more photogenic. It was too cold to go to the mall. A long, long day.

*

Nothing happened this morning. How can I be expected to live like this? Finally it was time to go out. Wore woolly hat, scarves and gloves. School was just getting out. Sang that line from 'Poison Ivy' over and over again to myself 'YOU CAN LOOK BUT YOU BETTER NOT TOUCH' I wonder if I have any musical talent. No one ever encouraged me. Got tube and bus to Miss MacDonald's office. It smelt of dirty clothes, like the library. She asked how I was.

'Bored and depressed.' What had I been doing? I was reading a lot, I said. Had I thought about my future? Had I decided on what interested me so that she could think about a course or some training? If I had something to do I wouldn't feel so bad. I gave a 'hollow laugh'. I must be interested in something she said and blushed. I decided to help her out. I said I'd given it a lot of thought and I was most interested in computers, photography and books. Perhaps I could go into publishing? I liked cooking and cleaning as well. Miss MacD. was very pleased. She said there were opportunities in all these fields, courses in word-processing and photography and book-binding – or even nursing! Had I thought of geriatric nursing? She promised to send me some brochures. And what about group therapy, had I thought that over too? I said what was past was past and I didn't want to dwell on it. She looked out the window for a while, into the darkness. All in all it was a good session but I was happy to leave. On the way home I pretended I was Dracula. I imagined going up to some children and saying 'Come with me to the land where all the sweets are shaped like skulls.' They are so excited and I wrap my cloak around them and we blast off like a rocket to my castle. It stands above the world on a mighty rock. It is made entirely of multi-coloured jelly sweets, shining like stained glass. And there in the mountains, together, we are free.

*

Got up for the postman but he didn't come. Miss MacD.
had sent nothing! It is just typical. I feel so bitter. I'd like
to get her for this. Honestly, some days I wish I was back
in prison. At least I had some company there. Not much
but a bit. They kept us out of the general population. We
never had any association time. You wouldn't believe
how much they hated someone convicted of my offence!
I'll never forget what they called me. 'Short Eyes'. Yes. I'll
never forget those screams in the corridor when I was
escorted past. 'Fucking Short-Eyes-Bastard Cunt' and
much, much worse. I couldn't write it down. Miss MacD.
says I should seek to understand my offence but there's
nothing to understand. After Mum's death all the kids in
the block liked to hang about at my flat because I was free
and easy. I had some imagination – not like their parents.
Anyway they only looked like kids. In their heads they
were older than me. The court couldn't understand this.
These children knew all sorts of stuff – sex stuff I'd never
heard of. I tried to straighten them out. I read them fairy
stories and told them about vampires and the undead and
all that. They loved it. Anyway there was this one little
tyke, Kevin, who just wouldn't leave me alone. He was a
real bother, always tormenting me and saying if I gave
him 50p he'd show me his thing and that's what I really
wanted wasn't it? Where does a kid learn to think like
that? I tried to laugh it off but he was really annoying. He
would hang around my place till really late. His parents
didn't give a toss of course – out all hours or smoking
drugs in someone's flat. So that one night I thought I'd
sort him out, teach him a bit of a lesson perhaps but mainly give him some responsible education about how boys
matured. I mean he was a menace – he could have raped
someone in a few years. Obsessed with sex he was.
Anyway there was a ruckus and Kevin started banging
around the flat like a panicked moth – the electric had

been cut off or I forgot to put the lights on. I don't recall. Somehow he broke some fingers. He wrecked my bathroom window and then his parents and all these druggy people with dreadlocks were screaming at my door. *I* had to call the police! And then they took no notice of this shower, staggering about outside like zombies. I even pointed out to the police that they could make several drug arrests but they took absolutely no notice. They were needling me, saying things like 'Led you on did he, the kid?' and laughing. Pig ignorant if you'll excuse the joke. But I was so glad to get out of there that I didn't even ask for bail. The estate had been going downhill for years. I didn't think much of the psychologists they called in while I was waiting for trial either. 'Poor impulse control' said the report, as if I hadn't been exercising more iron control and will-power in a day than they could have summoned in a century. Still, I did my time like a man. Afterwards I was relocated although one north London suburban housing estate looks much like another, I can tell you.

I have decided to forgive Miss MacDonald. She rang to say there was a big exhibition this weekend 'Welcome To The Working Week: Computer EXPO' and her office were prepared to pay for my ticket provided I registered for a course. This could be my destiny. I long to monitor the Dow Jones and the Nikkei. I felt excited all day. It sleeted in the afternoon so I didn't like to go out. I am strong but every sensitive person has a certain frailty. Read a book about Jeffrey Dahmer. He wore yellow contact lenses. Funny colour to choose. I'd go for a dark, mysterious green.

My ticket arrived but my good mood had gone. I haven't been to town since I got out. I haven't got the wardrobe.

Tried to trim my hair. I'll admit I'm nervous. I'll even admit I'm lonely. I smile at people but they don't respond. There's no way they can know about me here but I imagine they do. I imagine they can read my mind. Everyone has fantasies of course, I'm being such a silly. Still cold. Next door's Alsatian did its business on my steps again. Sometimes I wish I was a neutron bomb that could destroy all the adults and leave everything else, children, animals, the shops and cinemas, all the nice and beautiful things in the world.

The unbelievable happened! I found a friend! Everything is going to be different. Let me tell it from the beginning. It was sunny so I walked to the tube. There were lots of kids in the mall so I waved and some waved back. I started to feel good. I carried my shoulder bag with tissues, matches, purse and ticket although I left my pills at home. I never take them anyway. I bought *The Guardian* but just carried it under my arm. Had to change twice to get to Olympia. Unfortunately someone had altered the 'W' of 'WEEK' on the big sign to a 'G' which was a bit disrespectful.

The central hall was like a railway station, vast and domed. It seemed to go on for ever. What with the lights and bursts of gunfire and film dialogue from the screens I felt bewildered but started going slowly round the stands. Virtual reality was the best – I'd like to work in that I decided. Then I was a bit tired so I thought I'd have a break. I got a Fanta from a machine and started walking towards the rest area when suddenly I saw the most beautiful art. On two big screens were patterns that made me catch my breath. They looked as if all the rainbows and jewels in the world had melted into each other – a bit like my castle. The patterns sparkled and swept around – I could see orbs and crowns and lace and snowflakes in them. I walked up close and saw that the patterns seemed to go on for ever. There were paths in them that could swallow you up. I was 'hypnotized'.

'Psychedelic isn't it?' said someone next to me.

'Mmm,' I said, not looking round. 'What are they?'

'They're fractals. This one's a Mandelbrot and this one's a Julia.'

'They're so beautiful,' I said. 'So various.'

'They're infinite, but at the same time all that just comes from one basic pattern – one for each of these. One Mandelbrot, one Julia.'

'One Mandelbrot, one Julia,' I repeated, getting it right this time and finally turning round. I got such a shock! The speaker was an elegant, well-spoken young man but he looked like a villain. He was tall but thin, with silvery blond hair combed straight back. He was wearing Ray-Bans and a silver grey suit of impeccable cut. Underneath he wore a black T-shirt with 'Mr Bad Example' printed on it in small, precise letters.

'Tell me more about them.' I was pleading with my eyes, forcing him to respond. I have a strong personality even when thrown.

'Well – there's a shop near by. It specializes in this stuff.'

'Can we go?' I said, knowing immediately that I had sounded too eager.

'Oh – they probably have a stand here.' He was backing off.

I tried to act cool.

'Is there anywhere one can smoke here?'

'I think so but I didn't even bring mine.'

'Well I did. Where's the place?' I knew he was wavering so I sort of poked *The Guardian* forward and made sure he saw it. He'd know I was harmless and civilized. I knew it would relax him and it did.

'It's over there.'

I breathed again. He was the first real person I'd spoken to since I got out. I knew I had to hang on. When we lit up I offered him my Fanta but he wrinkled his nose and said, 'No cups.'

I could see he was eyeing my anorak and cords with disdain so I decided on a do-or-die psychological move.

'I know what you're thinking,' I said. 'I don't look too good but I just got released this morning. These are prison issue. No fault of mine.'

It worked! He wasn't to know that I'd have got my own clothes back at the end.

'My God,' he said. 'I just don't believe this! You got out this morning and you came here . . . That's just so amazing.'

He seemed really impressed. He shook my hand and introduced himself as Mark Firenzi saying that he was an artist and had a studio up the road in Kensington. Why didn't we walk round there? Well, this was a turn up for the books. Was he queer for villains? Watching my cords billow around my ankles as we walked I doubted it. This was a boy who cared for appearances. But he was still very interested in me and asked a number of questions. What had I been inside for?

'Just the usual. Robbery – pity I took the shooter along though!'

'Wow.' Had I had a hard time inside?

'Oh no – it was a doddle. Lot of old mates, job in the library. No one was going to give me any aggravation!'

I was well impressed when we reached Mark's residence. It was an entire house, just off Ken. High Street. We went into the kitchen on the ground floor although there was nothing there that qualified it as a kitchen to my mind. The table was made of metal and looked like a car-wreck. Mark managed to boil water in a retort stand and make some sort of rancid herbal tea. He sat down opposite me. He had taken off his sunglasses and I could see that his eyes were the exact deep green I would have chosen for my contacts! I took this as a good omen although I was feeling increasingly nervous. What did the guy want?

'Cheers,' I said. 'Well art obviously pays – not like crime!'

'Yeah, I do pretty well. You gotta know how to manipulate the market. It's all death stuff at the moment but I figure it's time for a change.'

Death stuff???

He leaned towards me, his eyes glassy and blank like perfect green marbles.

'What do you want most in this world? Mmm? Mr Faust?'

'It's Gavin actually. Well at the moment I'd settle for a bath, a change of togs and a visit to my old mum.'

Mark hit the table impatiently. He probably hurt his hand.

'Oh go have a shower then. Take some clothes. I mean, seriously, what do you want?'

I was pulled two ways. I needed new horizons yet something about Mark made me very uneasy.

'Same as everyone of course. I'd like to be rich and famous . . . I'd like to live like this. I'd like to . . . um . . . be like you.'

I had been diplomatic. It was true in that I'd like to be famous more than anything and have a big house but I wouldn't want to be an autocratic faggy little fuck like Mark, excuse my language. I was me and that was better.

Mark smiled and put out his cigarette in a candlestick.

'Come and see the studio.'

Well if downstairs was a space capsule the next floor was Dracula's castle. Several rooms had been knocked into one to make a huge studio. The shutters were closed and it was almost completely dark. All I could see were two photographs, on facing walls, blown up several times more than life-sized. There was a bank of church candles in front of each one, like an altar. One picture was of a black man with a sub-machine-gun and the other was a nondescript-looking white guy. I gestured towards him.

'Fire risk! Who's that – your father?'

'Jacques Mesrine.' He pronounced it in a very Frenchified manner. I was none the wiser anyway.

I started sneezing from the dust. There were a lot of objects covered in dirty sheets. It was like a morgue. I seemed to be walking on sand when, oh my God, I got all entangled with a huge bird. Mark pulled me back, none too gently.

'Don't step there.' He reached up, angled a spot and switched it on. I nearly passed out.

There, on the floor, in a bed of sand was a human rib cage. Perched on it was a stuffed eagle with a strip of bus tickets in its beak. There were travelcards in various colours scattered on the sand.

'It's called "The Commuter". It was a very early piece.'

'That's art? Where'd you get the bones? Drag someone off the tube?'

Mark gave me that thin smile again as if to say 'You fool'.

'Medical supply shop. It's quite usual. All this is very passé now. Come and look at this one. Let me switch it on.'

It was a lot better, just a glass box with two luminous green dice suspended in it as if by magic. Then another light came on and I saw that there was a second glass box around it. On its back was the illusion of a gun muzzle, pointing straight at the dice and thus at the viewer. Suddenly the gun seemed to go off and a shower of soot settled between the glass boxes and slid away. The gun fired again and a great glob of red stuff did the same. And again, only this time it was confetti and tinsel and sparkly stars that shot out.

'Pretty,' I said. 'What's that one called?'

'Oh God – I haven't thought of a title yet. It's a real worry – it has to be something just right or they don't take any notice now. "Downtown" perhaps or "Vice Pack". Or "Evil Is In The Eyes Of The Beholder"? I don't know. Christ I'm tired.' He switched it off and started for the door. 'Tell me more about prison.'

'You forgot the candles.'

'They burn out.'

I had the shower and took a lot of Mark's clothes because of course I didn't want my mother to see me this way, so I said. The jeans were too small at the waist so I had to choose baggy T-shirts. I got a leather jacket and an overcoat too. Mark leant against the door and talked all the time. What was I going to do now I was out?

'I don't know.'

Did I have a nickname inside?

'I was always known as Sharp Eyes or Sharpie. See, no one ever got the jump on me!'

Would I like to do a project with him? An art project? It would make me really famous.

'What sort of project?' The shower was on now and it was hard to hear. Basically as far as I could tell he was saying that the only area left unexplored in art was crime. Murderers were more famous than any artists now and if he could combine crime and art he would have it made. And so would I.

'You want to kill someone in a gallery?'

'No, no, no. I just mean a crime that is not a crime – that harms no one. Art crime.'

'But how does anyone see it – how does anyone buy it? Crime is secret.'

'We film it.'

I thought this over as I tried to pooch out the seat of my new jeans with my hand before struggling into them. It sounded clever and if Mark was some sort of big deal in the art world – as he seemed to be – and that crazy stuff upstairs had bought him this house, he must know what he was talking about.

'It would be revolutionary. Make all sorts of state-ments.' Mark was still droning on. 'Magazines, TV, inter-views. The big time.'

I came out of the bedroom stuffing clothes into a carri-er bag. Mark didn't even glance at me but drifted down the hall.

'Hey! What would you need me for then?'

I followed him back into the kitchen.

'I need you Sharpie because – ' he spat out some tobac-co – 'this is going to look like a real crime, at least at first, and I want someone there who's experienced, who can handle things. We're going to rob a bank – well, pretend to. I've got other people to help out, but they're art stu-dents. I need a hard man, someone I can depend on. A partner. We're having a meeting here tomorrow, at three. Stay, if you like. I always stay at my girlfriend's.'

Mark had to be unbalanced to tell me this. If I was the person he thought, I could have stripped the house. Or could I? There was nothing there except fitted units, clothes and books. Who'd want a rotting eagle? I was none too happy to hear of the girlfriend. Not that Mark was my type – far too old and no innocence there – but I still hoped for a friendship despite everything and who needs women around? Flabby, leaking things. Self-righteous too, the lot of them.

I felt overloaded with worry and excitement.

'S'okay. I must see my mum. I'll come tomorrow though.'

'Brilliant. Great to have met you. Divine providence I'd say,' and he gave me a lovely smile, a real one.

All the way home I composed this entry in my head and pondered everything. Surely Mark was the ideal friend – rich, successful, attractive, charming when he wanted to be. But he's so . . . weird, said my inner voice. All artists must be like that, I answered. I'd never met anyone remotely like him. He was my gateway to the future. Through him I'd certainly make the world sit up and take notice. Divine providence indeed, I thought as I trudged down Kenton Road, snowflakes in my eyelashes, past the church, a new red-brick shaped like a rocket for take-off to God. Next door's mutt had done it on my steps again but this time I banged on their window and shouted, 'Stitch up that dog's bum!!' but I don't think they heard.

It has been a big day. It has changed me. I'm too knackered to even make a cuppa. Bedfordshire for me.

I can't believe my life has changed so suddenly. Went back to Mark's house for the meeting, wearing his clothes and a pair of plastic shades clipped over my glasses. I thought I looked quite good although I felt Mark was treating me with a funny mixture of contempt and deference.

'This is Sharpie,' he said. 'A recent guest of HMP Highpoint.'

He introduced me to the others, sitting around the metal table. There was Desiree, Mark's girlfriend, a disagreeable little know-all with a crew cut, dressed in black leather, and two art student 'helpers'. Flagg was a baby-faced blond with gold hippy spectacles, and Dean was a muscular, mixed-race boy with his hair shaved off and a

T-shirt saying 'Young, Queer and Proud.' I felt right out of place and was dismayed to see Mark snorting white powder from a mother-of-pearl eggspoon.

I tried to lighten the atmosphere with a joke. 'Well – you lot don't need to talk. You can just read each other's T-shirts!' but they didn't laugh. They were dead serious.

There were diagrams all over the table and Mark explained more to me. They were working on a 'breakthrough' project for an exhibition. It was called 'Crime Of The Century', and they had the bank raid all planned. They had cased the bank in Hatch End, a rich, quiet suburb not far north of my house. They would perform the raid, tear up some money or something and Dean would film it.

'Won't we just be arrested – for disturbing the peace or something?' I felt anxious but they couldn't all be insane – could they?

Mark sighed.

'They don't arrest artists. We're not doing this for gain. We're not hurting anybody. There was this guy – this artist – who made copies of bank notes. They didn't arrest him for forgery. He just got hours of prime-time television; a real heavy sentence.'

They all laughed.

'But if it's just a film, I mean, why don't you act it? Do it with actors?'

Desiree spoke like a machine-gun.

'We've completed that part of the project. I've been an Edwardian family poisoner, dressed in fucking Laura Ashley with a pestle and mortar. Dean has raped me. We kidnapped Mark's ex and her wimpy pop star boyfriend. Flagg did some bestiality. We burgled Mark's father's house and did all the things they do, like crap in the fridge.'

'Please,' I said. 'I'm a professional.'

Flagg cut in. 'The point is – the exhibition will include video footage, photographs and blown-up stills. Plus trophies and memorabilia. Oh – and T-shirts. Some of the crimes will be "real" and some won't. People will have to work it out, see? That's what's important.'

Dean leant forward. 'What will you do Sharpie, when we've made the money?'

'Why not actually *rob* the bank? It seems simpler. Seriously, if I had money I'd like to open an orphanage. A decent one, not a shithole.'

Desiree gave a mean smile.

'God, villains! So sentimental. Always giving to charity and running boys' clubs.'

I glared. 'The whole thing sounds like a wank to me.' They liked that.

Everyone cheered up. I saw the tone I was expected to take.

'It's all right for you arty bastards, but what about me? I'm on parole.'

Desiree's voice softened.

'We'll look after you. It's all quite safe. And you'll get lots of attention and go straight and go to posh parties and someone will ghost your book.'

Patronizing bitch.

'I can write,' I said.

And so the plans were laid.

I've spent the last three days worrying and going to the toilet. What have I got myself into? Yet I can see no other way forward, no other way to get out of this place. I need power. I need money and fame. I have been given this one chance to leave my old life behind and fulfil my destiny. How can I not take it? I've spoken to Mark from a call box every day, by arrangement. He enjoys these criminal touches, like in films. Miss MacDonald called and I said I had registered for a word-processing course. I HAVE TO GET OUT OF HERE.

Now that it's all over I can tell the story of that fateful Thursday. It was, as Mark said, 'a nice quiet busy day'. We made our separate ways to the bank. I took the train to Headstone Lane and walked across the playing fields. I was wearing my only suit, my court suit actually, and carrying a briefcase. Flagg and I took up our positions, looking in shop windows. Dean and Desiree had arrived by car. Dean had quite a lot of equipment and was pretending to take photos of Desiree in the small park next to the bank. She had on a blonde wig and was posing like a model. No one looked at them. People went in and out of the bank, mainly women. It was a sunny day with signs of spring and the whole street was very quiet and ordinary in a leafy, pretty kind of way.

At 11 a.m. exactly Mark drew up in a long silver car and parked outside the bank. He pretended to read *The Times* for a few minutes, then got out, glanced around and walked quickly into the bank. Flagg and Desiree drifted in after him, casually. A couple of people left the bank and then Dean walked in too, cameras round his neck, carrying the camcorder. I waited a few minutes as instructed – an elderly couple and a woman with children entered the bank – and then when the street was empty, I went in. I shut the glass doors behind me and slid the deadbolts. I took the notice out of my case and stuck it up, 'SORRY – CLOSED 11 a.m. – 2 p.m. FOR ELECTRICAL REPAIRS & REWIRING'. I could hear a lot of noise from inside. I walked through the wooden inner doors, closed and barred them too and then turned to face chaos.

It was a small old-fashioned bank and the staff were not

completely enclosed by glass. Mark had got behind the counter through the side door and was waving his gun (*'They're not real ones, Sharpie'*) and screaming at the employees.

'Get away from those buttons NOW. This is NOT a raid, we won't hurt you. This is ART. SHUT UP!!'

Desiree and Flagg, with guns drawn, were covering the customers who were milling around in tearful hysteria. Dean was off to my right, in the shadows, fumbling with his equipment. I edged towards him. Suddenly a male employee leapt at Mark and Desiree fired her gun twice. (It *was* real.) The recoil knocked her backwards but the gun must have had a silencer. I heard it go 'pop'. Two glass screens shattered and everyone dropped to the floor. There was a strong smell of smoke and cordite. Total silence.

'Right,' said Mark, 'that's better. Just do as I say. You lot – up. Hands on heads.' He gestured towards the employees, who got up. Mark indicated they should join the customers. The male clerk tried to head-butt Mark as he passed him but Mark had reversed his gun and smashed the butt down on the guy's nose with such force that blood shot out and sprayed the shattered glass. The customers, some of whom had struggled to their feet, screamed until Desiree and Flagg advanced on them – then they shut up again.

Oh God, I thought, Mark's lost it completely. This is a disaster. I want out, or I'll be back in the nick. I remember thinking crazily, well at least I'll be a real criminal this time! Unobtrusively I joined the line of shaking customers.

The employees joined the others out the front.

'KNEEL DOWN!' screamed Mark and they all did. Mark then ran round to the tills, opened them and filled them with fireworks, leaving a trail of lighter fuel from one to the other. He took out a lighter and swoosh! the money went up in flames behind the glass – firecrackers and rockets flashed off, stars and purple rain shot up, fizzing and banging like crazy. A haze of gunpowder spread over the room.

'There!' gasped Mark, breathless. 'Do you understand now? We don't want your fucking money. This is art!! ART!!'

The customers whimpered. One old pensioner had peed his pants.

'Now I want it quite clear that this is art in action – art theatre. YOU are my material. I control you. Take off all your clothes and then we'll go.'

Humbly, stumblingly, totally dazed, Mark's victims started to remove their clothes. Some of them were crying. Mark smiled. Was Dean really filming this? I glanced over. He was being sick in a corner. I was standing next to a woman with two children. One, a baby, was in her arms and a toddler grasped her skirt, his little face white with fear. His mother was shaking so much she could do nothing. We were at the end, almost out of sight behind a marble pillar. I bent down and took off my shoes.

Desiree had started taunting an elderly lady who'd managed to pull off her dress.

'Ugly bitch! Gross! Get your knickers down!' – but it was when Mark darted forward and knifed open the old biddy's colostomy bag that I saw my chance. Everyone was in shock.

'Give me the children,' I said to my neighbour. 'They'll be safe. I can get them out. I promise.' I had taken off my jacket and of course I wasn't armed. There was a flight of stairs behind us.

'Softly, ssshh. Gently. I'll take them upstairs. Please. They'll get hurt here.' Her face was blind with panic but she managed, trembling, to give me the baby and bend down and whisper to the little boy. He took my hand. I smiled at the mother. 'Try to relax. I'll get help.' I drew the child away, towards the foot of the stairs. Mercifully he remained silent. As soon as I reached the bottom step I tucked the child under my other arm and ran like mad.

It must have been an old bell tower. The stairs went round and round, dizzyingly. Eventually I reached a sort of attic. It was a vast space with a glass roof, full of filing cabinets and dusty office furniture. The sun was flooding in and it was eerily silent. I could hear nothing from below. I put the children on a crate near a glass fire door. Opening it, I stepped on to a roof terrace overhung with trees from the park. The birds were singing and the sun felt very hot. I felt a strange sense of peace and power after all that insanity. I went back and managed to drag the crate out. The boy had got down and toddled after me.

'Look,' I said. 'Everything's all right now. See the birds?'

I picked up the baby. Was it OK? It had started to cry so it must be. I slid a finger down its nappy – just to check if it was wet or dry. It was a girl. I dropped it in an old flower tub.

I sat myself on the crate.

'Hey, what's your name then? Won't tell? Go on. I'll tell the birdies! HE'S CALLED JASON!'

The little boy giggled.

'The birdies say NO HE'S NOT!'

He giggled again.

'YES HE IS. JASON!'

'Timmy,' he whispered.

'Timmy, right! We've run away from the monsters haven't we, Timmy?'

'Monsters,' said Timmy. 'Mummy.' His face clouded and his little mouth started trembling.

'Timmy, Timmy, we're all right. Monsters all GONE. We're safe now. Oh come here, don't cry . . .'

I lifted him on to my lap. He was a very beautiful boy with dark blond hair cut pudding-basin style, big soft brown eyes and very dark eyelashes. He laid his head trustingly against my chest and I cuddled him, singing gently.

'It's all right now . . . it's all right now . . .'

That strange sense of deep peace and calm possessed me again. I even drowsed a little as I rocked Timmy. I felt as though I had taken on the world and won, as though he and I had fled a terrible battlefield and ascended into a pure and mystic heaven, a kingdom of my own. The sun poured down, the world was silent, the demons had disappeared. I was filled with a powerful sense of myself as sole monarch of the universe and gradually I became aware of a rising excitement. I had stolen this time from a foul world. I was a conqueror risen far above all the deception and madness that raged below. I started rubbing the little boy's tummy, easing his T-shirt up and his jeans down. His brightly-coloured trainers swung against my knee.

'Let's . . . just . . . see that you're all right now. Let's just . . . check you out. What a brave boy you are.' Timmy's eyelashes fluttered and he smiled as I manoeuvred him gently into the position I wanted.

'Now, we'll get a fire engine to check you out.' I unzipped my trousers and eased my thingie out. It was burning hot. With Timmy's back to me I positioned it under his bottom, between his bare thighs. I rocked faster. And faster as scenes from my own life started flashing through my head – *boys running – string in my hair – the teeth of the monster – bloodied flesh – the sting of urine – Mother shouting – the spurt and crackle as the big fire took hold – legs forced apart – feet drumming – bangs – Short Eyes! – lights, noise – Short Eyes!* – and I was gripping Timmy much harder than I intended and telling him it was all a game –

'Feel the fire engine . . . big fire engine, the fire engine's coming down the street . . . the fire engine's going faster, the fire's so hot and – '

Timmy squirmed and tried to turn round but I was jerked forward as an uncontrollable bout of pure excitement shot through me. Nothing could have stopped me now. As if from far away I heard the wind rising in the trees and the moaning of my own voice. I opened my eyes to see my offering – for that's how I thought of it – blowing across the rooftop like flecks of sea foam. And then the long wail of a police siren sliced piercingly through the morning air and I jumped up, swinging Timmy high into the air, fighting to control my voice and soothe him.

'Oh – whoah! Wow! Wasn't that funny? Hear the police cars? Hear the noise? Waawaah, waawaah! Come on, let's mop ourselves up – all clean now.'

As I lowered Timmy to the ground and started to straighten his clothes and use my tissues I took the time, despite my haste and fumbling, to tenderly kiss and nuzzle his private parts. I was fully aware of the poignancy – the delicacy – of our secret moments together. I kept talking too.

'All over now! We played a game didn't we? A fire engine game, a funny game?'

Timmy blinked at me.

'Funny. Fire emgine.'

Timmy smiled.

I was safe.

I hoisted the baby into the crook of my arm, took Timmy by the hand and we began the long, slow walk down. I can't say I was thinking very clearly at this point. I knew what I had done was wrong but it seemed the best way to comfort Timmy at the time and make him forget the awful things that had happened. And it worked! He felt the strength of my love and affection, he had been safe and protected. And that meant he'd forget all this soon. See, he'd forgotten already. Look at the way he was holding my hand and chattering on quite naturally, all his woes forgotten. No one could really say that what I had done was wrong, not if they understood the situation, the crisis. I had cared for him, saved him from the nightmare scene below. Anyone might have done the same. The noise grew louder as we descended – police radios, sirens, shouts – and when we reached the last step it was frenzy.

'Zandra – Timmy!' Their mother burst from a knot of policemen and took the baby. I hoisted Timmy to my shoulder and a battery of flashlights went off. Timmy began to cry.

'Stop that! You're frightening him,' I shouted and the photographers backed off. Timmy's mother reached up and put her arms around him.

'Timmy! Darling! It's all over. Are you all right, poor darling?'

'He's fine,' I said. 'I tried to soothe them and we played a few games.'

Timmy smiled at his mother.

'Monsters. Hot. Fire emgine.'

'OH GOD, I just can't thank you enough – I can't tell you what might have happened to them down here.'

'I know,' I said. 'I saw enough. The children would have been sacrificed to those people's craziness.'

A policeman held out my shoes, smiling warmly. 'That's right, son. Animals.'

Timmy's mother was crying. She kissed me on the cheek. Outside I could hear the high, excited voice of a television newscaster.

'I wish there was some way I could express my gratitude, Mr . . .?'

'Helier,' I said. 'Mr Helier. Gavin Helier.'
'May we have an interview, Mr Helier?'

. . . It was all over. Dean had obviously managed to creep out earlier because the police, on arrival, found all the doors gaping open. The other three were charged with everything possible from wilful destruction of property to assault with a deadly weapon. Mark, furious with Dean for not getting the fireworks on film, had done disgusting, sadistic things to his victims, until a cashier managed to nip round and press the alarm. No one was really physically injured except the guy with the broken nose but they were all traumatized. Timmy's mother had managed to hide behind the pillar but she couldn't have done that with the kids.

Mark turned out not to be a real artist at all but a neurotic rich kid who'd been in and out of hospitals and rehabilitation all his life. He'd apparently been playing around with art for a while, attending courses and such – not that he ever really fooled me, I must say – but his real obsession was crime and violence. These had fascinated him all his life. He longed to be a notorious criminal. He was already on probation for some pathetic drugs offence. The house and car belonged to his father. I learned it all from the papers. Flagg cracked up and was put in a bin but Mark and Desiree – infamous at last – got acres of coverage in the nationals. 'Art Crime – the New Menace?' 'Art's Bonnie and Clyde' and so on. Neither of them ever mentioned me or even Dean for that matter. I think they wanted all the attention for themselves, particularly after they sold the film rights. Mark was able to announce that he eventually intended to leave the country and found a cult – Religion–Art, he called it. Then they both vanished. Hopefully they'd learn how the other half lives. No one would stand for their nonsense in the nick.

As for me, there was a wonderful picture on the front page of the *Hendon Advertiser*, with Timmy smiling on my shoulder. 'Local Hero Saves Boy From Art Fiends'. I read the piece over and over again. It began 'Kenton photographer Gavin Helier (33) showed exceptional bravery when he rescued two local children, Timothy and Zandra Mann, from the clutches of an evil gang of "art criminals".' It went on to describe the raid and ended up 'Mrs Mann naturally wants Helier to photograph the children as part of the healing process and to cement a growing friendship. Helier comments, "Until recently my photography has been involved with long-term art projects, but now I think I have discovered a new interest in portraiture and will concentrate on that for the future."'

I had the sense to commandeer all Dean's cameras and claim that they really belonged to me. I picked up photography easily enough – it was very expensive equipment. I learned the rest from a book. It seems I have a natural talent. I explained to Miss MacDonald that the cameras had been left to me by a relative – fortunately she didn't check up – and that I'd been practising with them for some time hoping to surprise her with what was obviously my true vocation. I also felt able to open up and tell her, quite truthfully, how much the experience of witnessing a crime like that had shocked and sobered me. Seeing the awful effects of crime on the lives of private individuals, the pain and suffering that ordinary people went through when their world suddenly collapsed had made me much more mature. Miss MacDonald said she understood that the effects of my mother's death had overshadowed my life for a long time but that I now seemed ready to rejoin the community and that it was probably time to let bygones be bygones.

Well, that was three months ago. I got an incredible amount of local attention after the raid and Mrs Mann recommended to all her friends that I photograph their children too. The work poured in and I am just about to go full-time professional, specializing in child portraits and pets. I got a nice card made up too. At the top there is a photo of Timmy, his grandfather and the family labrador and beneath that curly lettering saying 'Preserve your tender memories – all of them!' and then two jokey inset pictures, one of some children all dressed up and throwing grass and mud on each other at a wedding and another photo of a huge litter of kittens climbing some curtains! Everyone says it is very cute and that I have a real way with all my subjects. I believe it is possible to say 'All's well that ends well!' I have enjoyed reliving some of my strange story but it's time to burn this notebook now I think!

Miss MacDonald has arranged for me to relocate to a lovely garden flat with space for a studio and a very large darkroom.

She is delighted with my progress.

Contributors

A.L.Barker has written eight collections of short stories and ten novels. She won the first Somerset Maugham Award in 1947, the Cheltenham Festival of Literature Award in 1963, and the S.E. Arts Creative Book Award in 1981. She has contributed to numerous short story anthologies and magazines and is a Fellow of the Royal Society of Literature.

Mary Flanagan was born in New England. Her short story collection, *Bad Girls*, was published in 1984, and she is the author of two novels, *Trust* (1987) and *Rose Reason* (1991). She lives in London where she is working on a new novel.

Damon Galgut was born in 1963 in Pretoria, South Africa. His first novel was published in 1982. It was followed by a collection of short stories, *Small Circle of Beings*, in 1988. For his second novel, *The Beautiful Screaming of Pigs*, he won the 1991 CNA prize. He lives and works in Cape Town.

Steven Kelly was born in 1965 and lives in London. He was shortlisted for the *Sunday Times* Young Writer of 1992 Award for his first collection of stories, *Invisible Architecture*. His first novel, *The Moon Rising*, will be published by Abacus later this year.

Born in 1923, **Francis King** has won the Somerset Maugham Prize, the Katherine Mansfield Short Story Prize, and the *Yorkshire Post* Novel of the Year Prize (for the bestselling *Act of Darkness*). His most recent publication is his autobiography, *Yesterday Came Suddenly*.

Deborah Levy's first novel, *Beautiful Mutants*, is published by Vintage, as is her most recent fiction *Swallowing Geography*. Her book of poetry, *An Amorous Discourse in the Suburbs of Hell*, is published by Jonathan Cape. She has been described as one of this country's leading experimental writers.

Shena Mackay was born in Edinburgh and lives in London. She has written eleven works of fiction. Her novel, *Dunedin* (1992), was awarded a Scottish Arts Council Bursary and shortlisted for the McVitie's Prize and the *Guardian* Fiction Award. A new collection of stories, *The Laughing Academy*, appeared last year.

Tony Peake was born in South Africa in 1951. He now lives in London, where he works as a literary agent. His first novel, *A Summer Tide*, was published by Abacus last year. His short stories have been included in *Winter's Tales* and the *Penguin Book of Contemporary South African Stories*.

Will Self grew up in London, where he still lives, and is married with two children. His collection of short stories, *The Quantity Theory of Insanity* (1991), two novellas, *Cock and Bull* (1992), and a novel, *My Idea of Fun* (1993), are all published by Bloomsbury. He is also a journalist and critic.

Ray Shell was born in North Carolina, USA. He studied acting, voice and play writing in Boston and since then has worked in theatre in America and England, has written, performed and produced music, and has appeared in film and television. His first novel, *Iced*, was published last year by Flamingo. He is currently working on a dramatized and a CD version of *Iced* and writing his second novel. He lives in London.

Barbara Trapido lives in Oxford. Her novels are *Brother of the More Famous Jack* (which won a Whitbread Award in 1982), *Noah's Ark* and *Temples of Delight* (short-listed for the Sunday Express Book of the Year Award in 1990). Her fourth novel, *Juggling*, will be published in 1994.

Elizabeth Young was born in Lagos, Nigeria, and educated in London, Paris and York. She is co-author of *Shopping in Space: Essays on American "Blank Generation" Fiction* (published by Serpent's Tail in 1992). A full-time writer and critic, she lives in London.